THE MOUNTAINEER'S PAINTING

A ghost story.

By David Francis Curran

Edited by Kaylie Burchfield & Patricia Ann Curran

©Copyright 2021, David Francis Curran

Disclaimer: All persons in this story are fictitious. Images of figures are models only. Any resemblance of the characters in this book to persons living or dead is coincidental. Ungacongagru is a fictitious mountain. There are climbing areas on Rattler Gulch Road in Drummond, Montana, but the monolith mentioned is fictitious. Daisy chains are real, however, the brand used here, a Subzero Daisy Chain, is fictitious.

I have included images of basic equipment in the chapters. There is a key to their identity at the end of the book, along with a guide to finding videos demonstrating climbing techniques and equipment online.

This book is dedicated to my Patty Ann—Patricia Ann Curran my wife, my lifelong editor and best friend.

DAY 1: SUNDAY

My name is Kevin Frost. I like to know what people look like in the stories I read, so I'll describe myself. I stand just a smidge over six feet tall, have wide shoulders, green eyes, and shortish red hair. I'm going to call this a ghost story, but I've never heard a ghost story like this.

The yard sale was out past the Forest Service office on Spurgin Road in the bowl of the Missoula Valley. It was hidden in the labyrinth of roads between the surrounding mountain peaks on which the snow still glistened in the sun. I would never have found the single-story ranch house but for the homemade cardboard signs with bright yellow arrows pointing the way. It was a warm Sunday morning in mid-May in the valley, and I didn't expect there to be a big crowd. The hand-made signs and the ad in the paper indicated it was the third day of a sale that had started on Friday. But when I pulled up under a large oak, there were no other cars parked along the road.

I wondered if there would be anything good left as I exited my car.

The offerings were the usual assortment of junk and collectibles plus more furniture than I would have expected. It seemed more of an estate sale than an ordinary yard sale. I didn't see anything at all that I liked until I entered an old, sagging mini-barn that had seen better days.

Propped up against the side of the barn, in a corner near the door, was a handsome wooden picture frame. Spider webs surrounded it. The thing had to be at least four and a half feet tall by three feet wide. The glass in the frame, for some reason, had been painted black, as had a metal nameplate at the bottom. I'd come across sandalwood once at a museum in the form of a carved Natraj idol. The finish of the frame had that same otherworldly gleam. There was no price. I leaned it forward so that I could look at the back. The back had been sealed in the way that professional framers do, with material stretched over the entire back. But in all the frames I've seen, paper was the backing material with the paper glued in place. Instead of paper, this one had woven cloth that appeared to have been stapled in place.

"I can let you have that for a very good price," a nasal voice said behind me.

It startled me so; I nearly let the thing fall back against the wall. The man who had spoken was reed-thin with a shaggy beard and unruly hair, a lighter shade of red than my own.

He stood about an inch taller than me. His eyes were as green as mine but behind thick glasses that made his eyes appear to bulge.

My garage sale instincts rose to the occasion. "Well," I said, holding the frame away from me as if it had a bad odor, "It's very nice, I'll admit, but why would anyone paint over the glass?"

"I don't know," the man said, coming over and looking down at it. "I got it at a garage sale myself some time ago. I think the fellow said it was of a relative he wanted to forget."

"I don't know," I said, giving the frame a little shake. There was something about his manner that made me think he was lying about how he came by the thing.

"There is no paint on the frame at all. Whoever painted over the glass and nameplate was meticulous. You could throw whatever it is covering up away and have a very nice frame," he added.

I liked it. I imagined the frame might be quite valuable and wondered if this guy knew that. Then it occurred to me that it might have been stolen, and it was covered least it be recognized.

I leaned the frame back where it had been.

He was watching me. As I turned to the door, he said, You can have it for $50."

"$50?" I said. It was a ridiculously low price for such a large frame made of one of the most expensive woods. "It's nice, but I only have $30 with me."

"It's yours for $30," he said. "May I wrap it for you?"

I looked at him. He had a strange expression on his face as if my buying the painting was a relief. I thought about trying to get him to go lower, but something held me back. The weird thought came to me that 30 pieces of silver was the perfect price for this purchase.

"No need to wrap it," I said. "I'll take it as is."

○

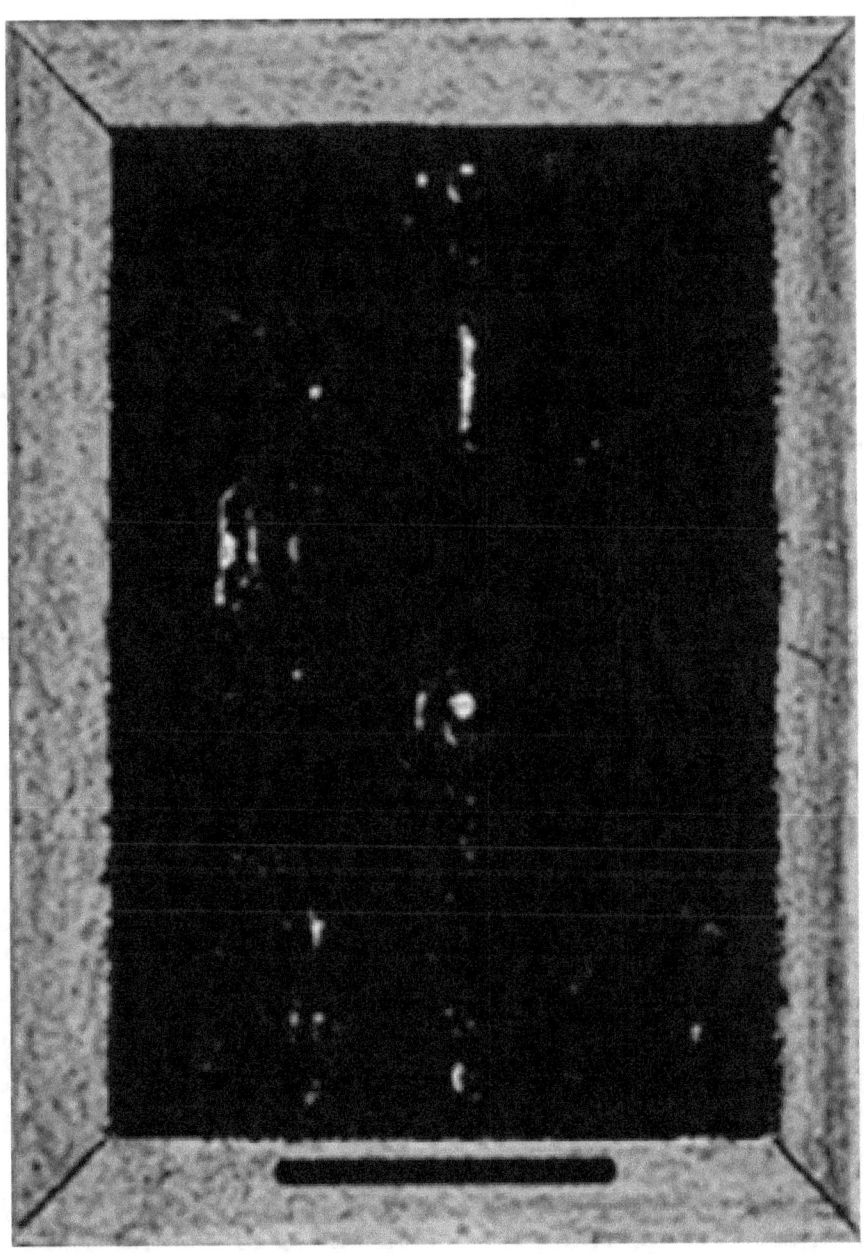

At home, I put the frame face down on the kitchen table. I used a pair of needle-nosed pliers to remove the staples holding the canvas-like backing onto the frame.

As I tugged with the pliers on the third staple, the staple flew out more quickly than I expected and nicked the finger of my left hand. A drop of my blood fell on the back of the frame and rolled beneath the backing. Afraid it would stain the wood, I wiped it off quickly with a wet cloth. I wasn't fast enough as my blood left a definite stain. At least it was on the back of the frame.

By the time I'd gotten all the staples out, I was ready for a break, but my curiosity got the better of me. I carefully turned the frame over with my hand on its back and laid it picture side up on the table. I then lifted the edge of the frame holding the glass down. The glass did not want to come free at first. I put my hand on the glass and applied a little pressure, and with a slight crack that made me think I'd chipped it, the picture and glass finally slipped out of the frame.

I moved the frame out of the way and lifted the glass. Instead of the visage of some frowning patriarch, I revealed a rather intricate double-matted painting. I believe it was a watercolor though I'm no expert. The outer mat was gray, with just the edge of the inner off-white mat showing. It was a complex scene. High above on the right, a sharp mountain peak stood sentinel beside turbulent mists that blended into a hazy sky. Beneath the peak, lower cliffs, green with tree-tops, skirted the mammoth peak like the dark hems of a dress.

At the base of the painting, a forest rose. Here the artist had given definition to the trees as if in the shadows of the trees, some depths could be made out, and paths could be taken. At the very bottom of the painting, so small I had to look closely to see, the painting was signed with three initials: T. I. F.

I rather liked it instantly and could not imagine why anyone would cover it up. Though I had intended to use the frame for something else, which I had yet to determine, I decided there and then to hang it up in my bedroom in a spot where I could see it from my bed.

o

Just before I turned out my reading light that evening, I glanced across the room at my new painting. It was easy to imagine being in that place, looking out at that lofty pinnacle from a distance.

DAY 2: MONDAY

°

I awoke the next morning from a dream in which I had been
hiking toward the very mountain in my painting. In my dream,
the morning air was chill, and as I made my way through the
primeval forest with a heavy pack on my back, I zipped my jacket
up around me. I was in a hurry because a group of people were
expecting me.

   As I drifted to wakefulness from my dream, my eyes fell upon
the painting that had inspired it. As I looked at it, it seemed there
were now areas of mist lower down in the picture. These mists

were moving as if stirred by a morning breeze. The impression was so intense I felt as if I were actually watching drifting mist. And then I felt a jolt as if catching myself falling asleep when trying to stay awake. I perceived what I thought was a pinpoint of reddish light shining at me from between the trees in the lower part of the painting. Alarmed, I got out of bed and went to the painting. As I moved across the room, the light dimmed, and the mists stilled. Yet, I now saw a change in the landscape itself. Previously, I had perceived the treed area near the bottom as devoid of any spark of color. But now, among the more defined trees, there where I had seen the glow from my bed, was a tiny daub of red that looked like painted-in firelight.

I wildly imagined that someone had broken into my home and changed the painting. But that was foolish. Who would want to do that? Besides, I hadn't shown the painting to anyone. I hadn't even mentioned it to anyone. The only one who even knew I had the painting was the man who sold it to me. But as I paid in cash, and he had paid no attention to me as I drove off, he most likely had no idea of who I was or where I lived.

After calming a bit, I reasoned that perhaps the minuscule speck of fire-glow in the immense landscape had been there all along. Maybe it had been covered by a speck of dirt which had been held by the glass when the glass was in place and had fallen off while I was out. I did keep the window open a crack for air. A breeze could have caused the change. That it seemed to glow with light was probably just an effect of a pinpoint of sunlight coming in on the side of my window curtains. That had to be it. It was the only possible explanation.

o

That day I was busy at work and got home late. From time to time, my thoughts had gone to the painting during the day, but I assured myself my explanation of the added detail had been correct. Once at home, I was so tired I barely gave a glance to the glow of the red fire in the painting before downing a quick nightcap of scotch in warm milk and climbing into bed.

That night I dreamed of approaching a camp lit by firelight. I was welcomed by a group of six—five athletic-looking men and one very fit-looking, lithe young woman with sky-blue eyes and light brown hair. The woman, almost as tall as I, rushed to me and kissed me. She smelled of lilacs. I noticed one of the men watching had an outraged look in his eyes over this display of affection. "I missed you," she said.

"I missed you too," I found myself saying. I wanted to add Patty Ann because I seemed to know that was her name, but I wasn't sure, so I said nothing. A bottle of whiskey that apparently was in the pack I carried to the site was opened, and the seven of us stood around the fire, lifted our glasses, and said with one breath, "To the climb!"

There were six pup tents set up. After the toast, the men each retired to one of them. The woman led me to the sixth.

In the tent, she kissed me on the lips and then said, "I've missed you, but we need to get an early start." She got into her sleeping bag, and I got into mine.

In the morning, we packed the tents and made sure the fire was completely out before grabbing what appeared to be climbing gear and heading out on a trail through the trees.

DAY 3: TUESDAY

°

As I woke, I tried to hold on to my dream. I'm a widower and have not even dated in the six years since my wife, Autumn, died of Rocky Mountain Spotted Fever after a tick bite. Autumn and I had been camping in the Scapegoat wilderness. Neither of us noticed the tick. It must have been brushed off soon after it attached itself. Unfortunately, when it attaches itself, it secreted the anesthetic to keep it from being noticed and the rickettsia group bacteria. When the spots and fever begin, you have very little time to get treatment. We were too far from help. I miss Autumn every day.

In the tent in my dream, the woman and I had simply held each other, fully clothed. I realized I had missed that level of tenderness, even if I was no longer comfortable with camping and the outdoors.

My eyes moved to the painting in my sleepy state, and again the mists rolled on the mountain. A brief time passed before I took in the painting as a whole. What I saw made my heart beat wildly with alarm. It might have been a bit unrealistic to think the tiny glow of the fire would stand out as it did when the sun had been hitting it, but its absence frightened me. I got out of bed and went to the painting. I examined it closely—the spot where I had seen the fire now held only the shadows of the trees. The red glow that I had seen as a campfire was now gone.

I didn't have time to dwell on it. I saw by the bedroom clock that I had lingered in bed too long and had an important appointment at work, but I was disturbed as I drove to work. The fire could not have simply vanished. A myriad of possible explanations ran through my mind. At some point, I finally asked myself: had someone painted the glass over because the painting seemed to change?

°

By the time I got home, I was almost afraid to look at the painting. A tiny speck of color could be rationalized as a minor thing. But somehow, I felt obsessed with it. In my bedroom, I found the painting unchanged from the way it was in the morning. In fact, it was the way it had been when I uncovered it, sans firelight.

I took a deep breath and relaxed a bit. Perhaps I had only imagined the red glow of a fire?

DAY 4: WEDNESDAY

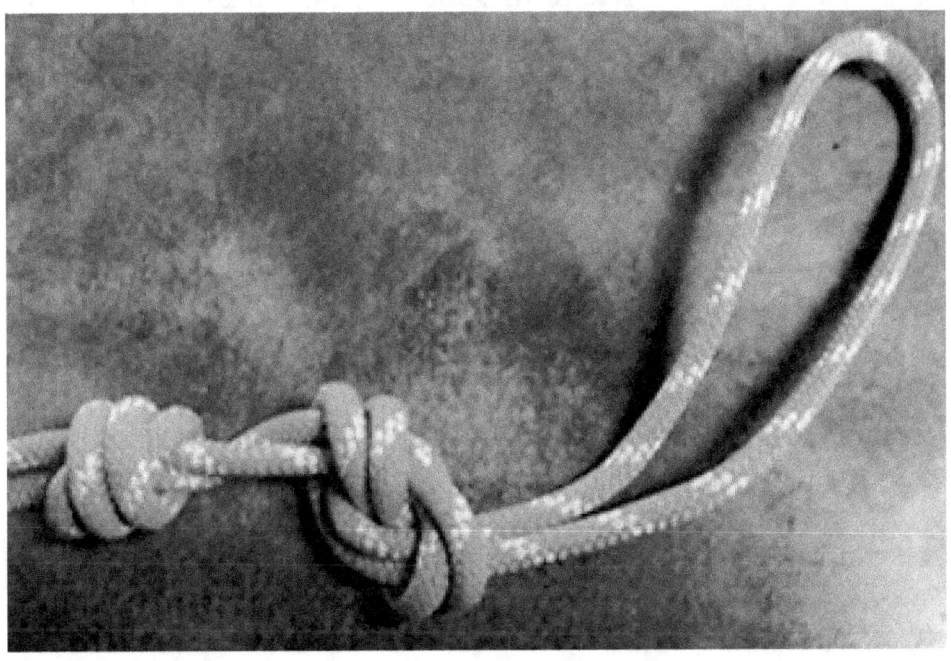

In the morning, I woke from a dream in which the other members of the group and I made our way through the last of the lower trees until we came to a staircase-like chute. Stone walls hampered our view, and as we climbed, we couldn't see anything but the sky above the chute.

On our first rest break, we sat on step-like stones, looking out from this three-sided chimney. I learned that morning that the woman's name was, in fact, Patty when one of the other men called out to her and asked, with a knowing wink, if she slept well.

So, I had been right the first time I saw her when I thought that her name was Patty Ann. It was as if a part of me was me in the dream, and part was the man she had welcomed as Tif. I hesitated to say her name when I met her in the earlier dream because I thought I might be wrong. But now I doubted I, as me, could add anything to the dialogue of the dream. I seemed to be following a script that had already been written. But the feelings I had in the dream, at least, were real to me. She may have been a stranger to me, but I seemed to have a warm longing for her company.

Patty came and sat next to me as I looked out over the astonishing view of sweeping green treetops, rock spires, and a distant gleaming lake. I watched as she took off her right glove then tugged on my left glove pulling it free. I found her touch warm and intoxicating as she held my hand for a moment sitting close enough that her side touched mine. She still smelled of perfume. Her breath whispered against my cheek for an instant, and then she kissed me there. I felt the warm, moist impression of her lips. The intimate touch was too soon broken as she'd picked up her water bottle, took a long drink, and then began to eat some granola. The spot she kissed grew chill in a rising breeze.

I found myself eating and drinking quickly, knowing that I had to keep my energy up and my body hydrated. I was done before Patty and took a notebook and pencil from my pockets. I found myself doing a fast sketch of the marvelous view before me. Patty leaned over and looked at it. She smiled but said nothing.

I had to admit surprise as I rose with the others to continue our climb and took deep lungfuls of the cold, clean air. Since I did not feel as tired as I knew I should feel after such a climb, I was definitely inhabiting a body other than my own.

Now the climbing group began roping themselves together. And I, to my surprise, slipped on my climbing harness as thoughtlessly as a pair of shorts. In fact, the harness looked like open-faced shorts with material only in the adjustable waist loop and two leg loops. The straps holding this combination together would not do for modesty if the harness was all one wore.

The group formed with the five other men in front. The man who had looked at me so angrily the night before was in the lead.

Patty followed the men. She smiled at me as she clipped onto the rope. I took up the final spot tying a--to me--complicated figure-eight knot that my hands tied effortlessly in my dream.

o

o

Now the path was no longer a staircase and rather a steep climb. I had to find hand and footholds and push and pull myself up.

This climb seemed to last hours before we finally reached a

plateau of somewhat clear level ground. Here the high peak in my painting was again visible. That peak was our ultimate goal.

Patty led me to a spot as far as possible away from the other climbers and whispered, "Let's set up here, so we have some privacy."

I pulled her to me and kissed her. She laughed and pushed me away. "The tent first," she said coquettishly.

o

As Patty and the man I was in my dream sat watching the sunset from the front of our tent, I took a small box from my inner pocket.

"I have something for you," I said.

"Really?" she asked.

I opened the box. The diamond of the engagement ring twinkled with sunlight in the thin mountain air.

"Yes, yes, yes, yes!" She cried.

The others in the camp looked our way.

"I'm getting married," Patty cried.

Four of the men gave us a cheer and a thumbs up. The fifth man's eyes seemed to be burning into mine with hatred.

When I looked back at Patty, there were tears in her eyes.

"You're crying?" I asked.

"I'm just happy," she said.

o

Mists swirled as if real in the painting as I came to full wakefulness. I don't ever remember dreaming in such detail. As Patty cried out with joy, I felt a thrill that she would marry me. But a sense of foreboding, probably due to the hostile glare of that one man, made me uneasy.

A glance at the painting showed me it was exactly as it had been with no hint of a fire.

I now felt something like an energy from the painting. Was I dreaming of events that had actually occurred? Was the woman in my dream real? I had to know more.

One nice thing about owning your own business is you can take off if you feel the need. I called my assistant and told her I would not be in that day, and I was leaving everything in her capable hands.

My first stop that morning was the house where I found the painting. I was not totally surprised to see a Realtor's sign advertising the home for sale. I parked by the same oak and went to the door. There was no answer to my knock.

I used my smartphone to do a reverse address lookup. It took me to a service that would provide the information for a fee. I paid the fee and was given the name and phone number of the owner of the house.

The name was Thatcher Ian Febbron. I wondered if this was my T.I.F.

I called the number and got a Verizon; 'This number is no longer in service.' message.

I did a Google search for Febbron. The first thing that came up was an obituary in the local paper. It was very brief. All it said about his death was that Thatcher Ian Febbron had died after an extended hospital stay. He had been twenty-nine years old. The rest was about family, his mother and father, a brother, and a fiancée, Patricia Ann Calloway. I saved the info, and since it was already 8:30 a.m. called the number on the Realtor's sign.

Peggy Appleby was free, and when I told her I was at the house, she asked if I could wait while she swung over to show it to me. Her office was not that far away.

She suggested I look around the outside while she was en route. She mentioned the large backyard and the old mini-barn, which could be torn down.

I started off heading away from the old barn and walked along the far side of the house, which offered newish siding and a wire fence separating it from the next property.

o

°

Because the fence surrounded it, I could see the backyard was quite extensive. In the center of it was what looked like a stone pillar of some sort. A closer look revealed that the tower, which had to be 16 feet tall, had various shaped rocks protruding from its face.

Metal poles with pulley-like devices at their apex rose from the top of what I realized was a climbing tower.

The siding on the back of the house looked new, like that on the house's side. A large picture window and four skylights revealed the painter's studio. As there was nothing else of interest in the backyard, I headed over to the mini-barn.

The barn really was in poor shape. A man-sized hole gaped in the center of the roof. Roofing material dangled down, pushed inward by the elements. Beams of light coming through the hole lit columns of dust motes.

o

The building wasn't very large. I walked to a sort of closet in one back corner and saw the remains of an old feed bag on the floor. Something hung on the wall and I touched it. It was a canvas bag. I lifted it, felt a bit of weight, and looked inside. It contained flat steel spikes with open loops at the tops that I was unfamiliar with, and carabiners which I was familiar with. Carabiners are closed oblong steel loops with a lockable spring gate. Autumn and I used carabiners for hooking our tent's guy lines to loops on its stakes. After seeing the climbing tower in the back I assumed the two items were used in climbing.

As I was putting the bag back, I saw more items hung behind it. I pulled out two ice axes and two helmets. To my surprise, one of the helmets, an orange one, was similar to the one I'd dreamed I put on. The smaller helmet was yellow just like the one Patty had worn in my dream. A deep dent ran across the front of the orange helmet. Turning it over, I saw what might have been dried blood on its straps. I was looking at the straps when I heard a vehicle pull up outside. After putting the items back, I walked out into the sunlight.

o

The realtor was a short stout woman, with shoulder-length brown hair. She moved so quickly from her Subaru toward me, she seemed to exude energy.

"Peggy Appleby," she said. "You must be Kevin Frost?"

"Yes," I replied. "The outside is nice. I don't know if I'd ever use that climbing tower in the backyard, but the yard is spacious."

Peggy laughed. "That rig is not something every homeowner needs. But I'm sure you could find someone to take it off your hands. The previous owner's fiancée is a grade schoolteacher, and the two of them started giving climbing lessons to some of her students. Those lessons grew into a small climbing school in their backyard."

"I understand that he's deceased?" I asked.

"Unfortunately, yes." She replied.

"How did he die?" I asked. "I heard he was in the hospital for a long time. Was he ill?"

"No," Peggy said. "He had a climbing accident. He was in a coma for almost a year, and then he just died this month.

"Normally, the house would be tied up in probate for another year. But he had his affairs set up in such a way that should he die, the house would be available to his heirs to dispose of immediately. He knew how dangerous climbing could be."

"Smart move," I said. "I understand he was also a painter?"

"Oh, yes," Peggy exclaimed. "He is a rather famous watercolorist. His paintings are incredibly realistic. I wish I had one of his paintings now. His paintings were selling in the 10 to 20 thousand dollar range before he died. They began getting pricier while he was in a coma. They will probably skyrocket now that he is dead."

Peggy's revelation took me by surprise. That he was such a successful painter, and that his paintings sold for so much, explained the expensive frame I'd found my painting in. But if it was worth that much, why had I been able to buy it for only $30?

"Shall we go inside?" Peggy asked.

A light breeze stirred the air and I felt a chill. I nodded and followed her.

The interior of the house seemed to be mostly bare. Only a modern refrigerator, a stainless-steel stove and a new washer and dryer remained.

"How did you find the house," Peggy asked as we walked back through the living room toward the front door.

"I was here for the yard sale and met a red-headed man. Was that the brother?"

"Yes, that was Timothy. He came into town to help dispose of the household items," Peggy said.

"So he doesn't live in Missoula?" I asked.

"No, Helena. He tried staying in the house. But, apparently, it was too painful for him. He spent the last few days, while the yard sale was going on, at a local motel," Peggy said. "He did manage to dispose of almost everything. The rest he donated to Goodwill."

So, the brother lived in Helena. I decided then and there to call him, and, if he were home, drive there that afternoon. I wanted to talk to him again, in person.

We moved into the room with the picture window and skylights. The floor was bare polished oak, and white paint covered the walls. I notice some color stains on the floor in the center of the room.

"He was a painter," Peggy said. "So some paint did fall on the floor. But the floor is oak and can easily be sanded and refinished."

"I don't know if I would touch it," I said.

"So will you be selling your home by Blue Mountain, Mr. Frost?"

So, Peggy, it seemed, had done some research on me. It gave me a twinge of guilt as it reminded me, I was wasting her time.

I paused, probably too long, and figured that she might think I was going to lie.

"I'm just looking for investment property, really. Something about this place intrigued me when I came to the yard sale. I don't know why. If I do decide to do anything about this house, I will give you a call."

"Thank you," Peggy said. "I do have other investment properties...."

I endured the time it took for her to try to convince me she was my best option for real estate investments. It was the least I could do. We left it that she would email me her listings.

I found Timothy Febbron's address in Helena and called him. I told him I had some questions about the house that Peggy Appleby couldn't answer. He tried to get me to ask him on the phone, but I said I'd like to look the estate executor in the eyes when I asked. I then lied and promised him that since I liked the house a lot if he could satisfy my inquiry, I would be able to pay cash. He agreed to see me for lunch, my treat, and named an Irish pub that I had heard mentioned as a great place to eat. We'd meet there at 1 p.m.

The look on Timothy Febbron's face when I walked up to the table where he waited for me was one of unhappy surprise.

"You?" He said, standing.

I guessed he thought I had come to discuss the painting, and he obviously did not want any part of that.

"I really liked your house when I saw it," I said. "I had thought of getting myself something in a quiet neighborhood, and when I found out that it was for sale, I asked to see it."

The man relaxed and sat back down. "It was my brother's place. He recently died, and I had to put it on the market."

"I understand. And my sympathies for your loss," I said assuredly. "But I find it unusual that a property can be transferred so soon after the owner passed away. I am a little concerned about probate causing me a problem in the future."

I was astounded at how easily I was lying. But I sensed in his uneasiness that Timothy Febbron was trying to conceal something. I needed to get to the bottom of the experiences I had been having in my dreams and the changes I was seeing in the painting.

"Thatcher put the house in a corporation rather than under his own name. My parents, his fiancée, and I are the only shareholders. I am the executor. There is a clause that states that if one of us should die, the corporation will go to the remaining shareholders," Timothy explained. "So there should be no problem at all."

"Could you send me the articles of incorporation, so my attorney can check it over?" I asked.

"No problem," Timothy said.

"One other concern," I said, "He was engaged? I heard her name is Patricia Ann Calloway?"

"Yes," Timothy said. "He was engaged to Patty Calloway, and she is one of the shareholders, but you don't have to be concerned that she will claim the house. We actually offered it to her, and she refused it. She lived there with my brother, and the place had too many memories for her. My brother had a substantial accident insurance policy of which she was the sole beneficiary. She will also inherit all his unsold paintings. So, she has been well taken care of to the extent that the sale of the house is of little consequence to her." He had a sudden look on his face as if he had just said something he shouldn't.

"I didn't know when I went to your yard sale that your brother was a well-known painter," I said casually, trying to sound like it was just an aside. The look on his face let me know I'd hit pay dirt. "If that was one of his paintings that I bought, it could be worth a great deal of money."

"You haven't looked at it?" Timothy asked, surprised.

"No," I said. "I bought it for the frame. But considering it was at his house, could it have been his?"

I watched him carefully. He had told me that he had picked it up at another yard sale. I wondered if he remembered that.

"I suppose it could be," he said. "My brother had some quirks, but why he'd paint the thing over, I don't know."

"Well, I am interested in the house." I lied; since he had just lied to me, I felt no guilt at all. "I'd like the documentation we just mentioned. And," I paused. "Is Patty Calloway still living in Missoula? I'd like to reassure myself she has no claim on the house, nor any intentions toward establishing one."

Timothy gave me a pained look. "Yes, she was when I last heard from her. She's a teacher at one of the schools, so I assume she is still around.

"Do you have her contact info?" I asked.

"I can text you her new phone number," he said. "I don't think I have her current address."

º

I decided I needed to think about how I would approach Patty Calloway. Thinking about her made me remember the kisses of the woman in my dreams. Did the real Patty Calloway resemble that woman? I hadn't been to Helena in some time and decided to stay overnight at the Sanders Bed & Breakfast. My wife and I had stayed there before she died. It had been a happy time.

I slept through the night without dreaming. I assumed it was because the painting was back in Missoula.

DAY 5: THURSDAY

°

I woke at 9 a.m., which was late for me, and called my assistant in Missoula and told her that I would not be coming in today. I then used my iPhone to look up a reverse phone directory. It gave me an address for Patty Calloway in Missoula that was not the house where I'd bought the painting and frame.

I hoped it was a current address. I decided to pay for some of the additional information that the site had for sale.

Apparently, Patty Calloway was a grade schoolteacher at Blue Mountain School. It was a coincidence. Autumn and I had bought our home so that our children could go to that very school. I had no idea if Ms. Calloway was still working, but if she was not at the address I'd found, I could try looking for her at the school. After enjoying some juice and waffles, I left Helena and headed back to Missoula.

o

There was no answer when I knocked at Patty's door in a neighborhood not far from Patty's school. Hers was a pretty red house with a white picket fence in a middle-class neighborhood not that far at all from my own home. I wondered if she was renting it. An older woman in a white dress emerged from the house next door on the right. She was headed to her car, which was parked out front.

"Hello," I said cheerily," I was wondering if you could help me."

She stopped and looked me over with bright blue eyes. She had dark hair going gray in a short, attractive hairdo. I wondered if she thought I was a bill collector or process server as I was dressed in my jacket and tie.

"Does Patricia Calloway still live here?" I asked, smiling. "I'm from her late fiancé's insurance company."

She smiled then at the lie.

"Yes, but she's not home," the woman said, offering no more to a stranger than was polite.

"Is she still at Blue Mountain School?" I asked.

"She usually gets off at three. She used to stay for band. She's the music teacher as well as the sixth-grade teacher, but they had to let band go because of budget cuts."

"Thank you very much," I said. And she drove off.

o

I found the school office. The woman at the desk, who I took to be a receptionist, asked, "Can I help you?" as she stood. She had a pale yellow pants suit on and looked to be in her late twenties or early thirties. She had brown hair tied back in a ponytail. Her eyes, I saw as she came near, were a shade of light brown.

"Is Miss Calloway still in charge of the band?" I asked.

"Yes," the woman said, nodding her head. "Although we have had to suspend band for a while due to budget problems, as well as all other of our after-school activities.

"But they will be starting up again shortly."

"I hadn't heard about the problems, but I'm glad they are starting up again," I said, taking out my checkbook. "I do hope you can restore band practice sooner rather than later. And I promised my wife I would leave a contribution."

The thought of Autumn tugged at my heart. I knew she'd forgive me the white lie I'd just told and approve of my donation.

"Well," the receptionist said. "Thank you."

I wrote a check for 1,000 dollars and handed it to her.

"Wow," she said. "Well, thank you again."

"Is miss Calloway here today?" I asked.

"Yes," the receptionist said. "She's in class now; she also teaches 6th grade."

I looked at my watch. It was one o'clock. "I'd like to wait for her. Outside, of course. What time will she be done?"

"We are ending at two today," she said and looked at the clock behind her on the wall above an inner door. "So you'll only have an hour. I'll tell her you wanted to see her. If you need to do something else and can come back, I can ask her to wait."

"I'll just wait," I said. "Thank you."

She didn't ask me my name, but, of course, it was on the check I just wrote. I was parked across the street, so I could easily watch the front door. As I waited, I called work which was a mistake. Apparently, there was a pressing problem that only I could solve. I promised to be there as soon as I could.

As the students began to exit the school, it occurred to me, again, that I really didn't know if Patty Calloway looked like the woman in my dream.

Even if she did, if her hair had grown longer, and she dyed it, I might not recognize her from a distance at all.

But just moments later, my heart began pounding in my chest. My head felt dizzy. A tall woman, seeming to tower over the small children who swarmed about her, was moving toward me. Her face and hair seemed to be exactly like that of the Patty from my dream.

I exited the car and began walking toward her. She came toward me. A moment later, I could see she had beautiful blue eyes, the same eyes I looked into in my dream.

"I assume you are Kevin Frost?" She asked.

"That's me," I said. "And I'm guessing you are Miss Calloway?"

"Yes," she said. "Tim called me and told me you would be contacting me. Though you didn't need to come in person, I could have told you over the phone that I don't have any designs on the house."

"Mixed memories?" I asked.

She nodded. "And since Thatch left me very well off with insurance and his unsold paintings, I don't have any need for anything from the sale of the house. I thought his family should have something."

I felt a sudden fear our conversation was almost over. Patty'd answered the question I was supposed to be here asking. I scrambled quickly to find a way to continue the conversation. Luckily, she continued it.

"I do want to thank you for your donation to our band," she added. "That was very generous of you. I wonder if I could ask you about that donation?"

"My late wife and I picked this neighborhood for your school," I replied, embarrassed that she might be suspicious as to why I had made such a large donation. "When I asked for you, the receptionist mentioned that band had been suspended for a while.

My wife would have wanted me to help the school we hoped our children would go to."

I wasn't able to hide my emotions when talking about Autumn.

"I didn't mean to question why you made the donation," Patty said apologetically. "I meant to ask you about how we might use your donation. And I'm sorry for your loss."

I nodded. "I'm sorry for your loss," I said. She nodded back, and then we both stood looking at each other awkwardly for a few moments.

"I'll be honest," I finally said, breaking the silence. "I didn't need to talk to you about the house. But I really need to ask you about something I purchased at the sale at the house on Sunday. Frankly, it's something that's disturbing me a great deal."

A puzzled look crossed her face. "The yard sale Tim ran?" she asked.

"Yes," I said. "Something I discovered when I went to see Tim this morning that he hadn't been fully honest about."

"What was it?" She asked, curious now.

"It's not something easily explained. It will take a while to tell the whole story, and you said you want to ask me about how my contribution will be used. There's a problem at work, and I have to get back. Is there some way we can get together later?"

We decided to meet that evening at a new restaurant that I'd heard about and wanted to try.

°

o

I stopped home to change. When I went into my bedroom, I found that the painting had changed again. A single red glow stood out like an actual light hidden among the trees near the center of the landscape. This was an entirely new location. It was as if the campfires were following the climbing group in my dreams. I felt dizzy. I thought again that I was imagining things. As I changed my clothes, I kept my eyes away from the painting. But I had to look again before I left. The fire glow was no longer shining like a light, but it was still there.

o

o

I arrived first and was seated in a secluded alcove. A short time later, the host brought Patty over to the table for two.

"Can I offer you cocktails?" The host asked.

"Not just yet," Patty said. "I'm not sure if I'm staying." She did not sit down.

"I'll send a waiter in a few minutes," the host said evenly.

When the host left, Patty turned to me and said, "I don't want to offend you, but I seem to have reason not to trust you. So, I don't know if I'll be having dinner with you."

"Can I ask why?" I asked, my voice for some reason trembling.

"Can I ask you, Mr. Frost," she said in a calm no-nonsense tone, that I could imagine she used in her classrooms with misbehaving children, "why you told my neighbor that you were an insurance agent seeking me out about Thatch's estate?"

That she was a strong and smart woman was obvious.

"So she wouldn't think I was a bill collector," I said with a laugh. Patty did not smile.

"I was desperate to talk to you, and I needed to know where to find you," I added, honestly. "I bought a painting at the yard sale. Someone painted the glass over. I bought it for the frame. I took the glass off. It is a beautiful painting of a mountain, signed T. I. F."

"Someone painted the glass over?" Patty asked.

I nodded.

Patty's eyes went wide. A waiter was coming over. Patty pulled her chair out and sat down.

"Would you like to order cocktails?" The waiter asked as he handed us each a menu.

"I'll have a white wine," Patty said.

"A rusty nail for me," I said.

"I'll be right back," the waiter said and left.

I noticed Patty had a questioning look in her eye. I smiled back.

"A rusty nail?" she asked.

"I discovered the drink in college. Why?" I asked.

"It was Thatch's favorite drink," she said. She thought a moment, then asked, "Do you have any idea why it was painted over?"

"That's what I want to talk to you about. All I know for sure is that it's a watercolor of a mountain. And ever since I uncovered it, I've had dreams about mountain climbing. I have never been interested in mountain climbing. I'm afraid of heights."

"Well, most of Tif's paintings include mountains. The painting must have sparked your dreams," she said. "Were they just general dreams about mountain climbing?" she asked. I sensed a keen interest behind her question.

For a moment, I wondered if she were dreaming about the same thing. I had just met her and did not know her at all. To mention the intimacy I'd had with her in my dreams seemed inappropriate. While I wondered what to say, a silence hung between us.

Finally, she said, breaking the awkward silence, "but I can't imagine why one of Tif's paintings would be painted over. Can you describe it?"

"Well, I guess I'd describe it as brooding," I began. "Storm clouds and mist hover near a sharp pinnacle on the upper right...."

"I think I know the painting you mean,' Patty said, interrupting me. From the look of shock on her face, I guessed that the fact that it was that particular painting disturbed her.

"Tell me just how you came to buy it?" She asked.

So, I told her of finding the expensive-looking frame with the glass painted over in the mini barn. "I took it home and found the painting.

"I'm guessing that you weren't the one who painted it over?" I asked.

She seemed almost subdued. "The only one who could have done that is Timothy," she said. She thought a moment. "Did you ask Tim why it was painted over?"

"Exactly," I said. "I asked when Tim asked me if I wanted to buy the frame, why the glass was painted over. He said he didn't know as he had gotten it at a yard sale himself. Later, when I went to his house in Helena, he must have forgotten what he had said at the yard sale because this time he told me Tif must have painted it over."

"The painting was hanging in the house when I moved out soon after Tif died," Patty said. She wiped a tear from her eye. "It had not been painted over when I left. Because it was of the mountain where Thatch had his accident, I didn't want it. Bad memories. I left it thinking the family might want it. But I have no idea why Tim would paint it over. If you're wondering if one of us would want to claim it, you needn't worry. If Tim sold it, he obviously didn't want it either.

"I'm not worried about you or Tif's family wanting it back," I said and took a deep breath before continuing. "It's not just about having dreams of a climb up that mountain."

She looked at me intensely for a moment. The waiter came back. "Ready to order?" He asked.

I looked at the menu. "Chateaubriand for two?" I asked Patty.

She nodded.

"How do you like it?" I asked.

"Rare," she said.

"Chateaubriand rare," I said.

We didn't need to order hors d'oeuvres for as soon as the waiter stepped away, a girl came with an hors d'oeuvres's tray, and we both picked stuffed mushrooms. There was something almost otherworldly in our similar tastes.

But then I realized I was just fantasizing.

"I have dreams based partly on movies I've seen or books I've read all the time," Patty said. There was something odd about the way she said it. "I don't think it means anything. You saw the painting and had a dream about it."

It almost seemed as if she were trying to convince herself that my dreams didn't mean anything. I wanted to ask if she ever dreamt about, not the painting, but that fatal climb, but thought now wasn't the time.

I looked her square in the eyes. "The thing that bothers me is that the painting changes," I said.

Patty looked at me strangely. "What do you mean changes?" She asked.

I realized this was my chance to give her a glimpse of what I had actually dreamt without having to go into the intimacy I'd felt toward her. "That first night, after I'd uncovered and hung the painting, I dreamt that I was walking through a forest with a pack on my back to meet some people. That was Sunday night or Monday morning.

"But the next night, I dreamt I was approaching a campfire. When I reached the camp, there were six people there, we were all going to do a climb, and I was the last to arrive."

I noticed her expression changed when I said I was the last to arrive. It was as if I had stirred a memory.

"You said you were familiar with the painting?" I asked. "We're there any indications of a campfire in the forest?"

"No," she said, shaking her head.

"There weren't any indications of a fire when I uncovered the painting from under the painted over glass," I said. "It was just a landscape. When I woke the next morning, the mists on the mountain seemed to be moving. That could have been just a remnant of my dream. However, what was not a dream was that the painting had an added feature. I could see the clear glow of a tiny campfire in the forest near the left bottom of the painting. When the mists stopped moving, and I was fully awake, the fire was there."

Patty looked at me for a long time.

"I thought it was something some dirt had covered up. And that the dirt had somehow fallen off. But the next day, the fire was gone," I said. "It scared me; I thought at first someone was messing with me.

"The painting was back to normal until today," I said. "And today, it was changed again. This time there was a fire higher up on the mountain."

"You must have imagined it, she said.

"Maybe," I said. "That would actually be a relief."

She didn't say anything. The waiter brought our food just then, and we divided the meat. I thought it's time to change the subject.

"So what was it you wanted to ask about my contribution to the school?" I asked after a few bites of our meal.

Patty smiled. I looked at her and felt myself feeling dizzy again. She was a beautiful woman. Her perfume smelled like lilacs. It was the same scent from my dream.

"As I mentioned," she began, "I received a rather large inheritance when Thatch died. The insurance payment alone was big enough that I contributed to my school's band to the extent that they will be in good shape and able to start up again next week.

"So I wondered if you'd allow your donation to go to a fund we are setting up for one or more of Missoula's high school bands to go to the Rose Parade in Pasadena if invited. I also help out with the high schools, and that is a fund I hold dear."

"No problem," I said. "In fact, if you let me know when and if they are invited, my company might be able to fund the entire trip."

Patty smiled at me. "What exactly is your business? If you don't mind me asking. Not insurance, I take it?"

The waiter appeared and asked if we needed anything. I looked at Patty, and she shook her head, no.

"Not right now, thank you," I said.

As the waiter walked away, I looked into Patty's eyes.

"No," I said, "And I am really sorry about lying to your neighbor. I run an online newsletter offering free and bargain books. Do you read Kindle or Nook or Kobo books?"

"Yes," Patty said.

"Well, authors pay us to send out ads for their books which are on sale or free on Kindle, etc. We have over 8 million subscribers who receive notices depending on their taste in books. I have a small staff of 4, and we do quite well."

I told her the name of my company.

"I subscribe to that," she said. "That's your company?"

I nodded.

"When my neighbor told me you told her you were with the insurance company, I thought that you might be a con man or thief after my money," Pat said.

"I'm glad you still came," I said.

"You seemed sincere about something from the yard sale bothering you. So, I was curious," she paused and looked directly into my eyes. "And since I'm in charge of money for the band, I got to deposit your check in the band's bank account. We have the same bank. Your check was good."

o

We said goodbye in the parking lot. I didn't think I'd see her again. Just before she drove away, she rolled down her window and said, "It is funny. I've been dreaming about that climb myself." With a wave, she was gone.

o

On the way home with my share of the leftover Chateaubriand in a doggy box, I realized I probably wasn't going to get any further with the mystery that was the painting. If Patty had no idea who had painted it over, and Timothy was going to lie about it, I probably wasn't going to learn anything more about the painting.

In my bedroom, the glow of the second fire was still visible in the painting. I got my iPad and photographed it. Then immediately went to my photos and examined the image. To my relief, the fire was visible in the photo. Somehow I thought it might not be there.

And then I just felt sad. I thought of tall, beautiful Patty Ann Calloway sitting across from me in that restaurant, and the fact that I would probably never see her again and felt an emptiness I hadn't felt since Autumn had died.

DAY 6: FRIDAY

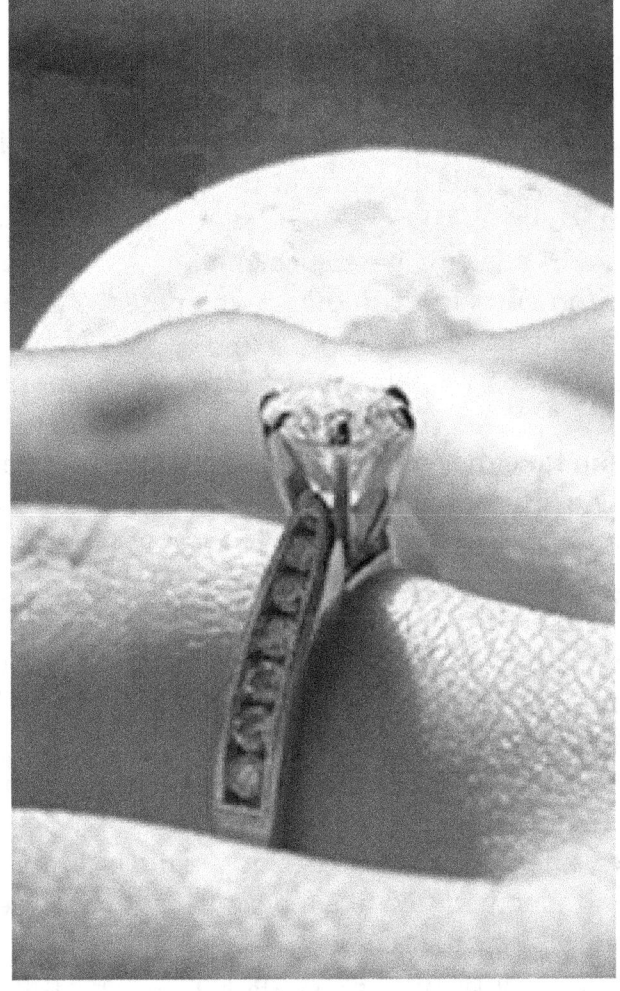

o

I awoke from a dream in which Patty and I were in our tent on the mountain. We'd zipped our sleeping bags together. A strong breeze was ruffling the sides of our tent. I realized I was naked. A delightful warmth spread over me. Patty was on my left, and I guessed she was naked too. She held her engagement ring out and was looking at it in the light that bled through the canvas of the tent.

"Good morning," I whispered close to her ear. I knew, somehow, it was a rule in our group that we try to be quiet in the morning so as not to awaken anyone who needed more sleep.

She turned to me. Her smile made my heart flutter. "You had it engraved?" she asked. "I can't quite read it in the morning light."

"You could go outside and read it," I whispered back. Some voice other than my own speaking.

"Stark naked?" she whispered back.

"I don't mind showing you off," I whispered. That voice inside again taking control.

She punched me in the arm. "Just for that, no morning fun for you."

"It says: You take me ever higher. All my love forever, Tif," I said and started kissing her ear lobe.

She turned and kissed me on the forehead. "I love it."

"So is early morning nooky back on the table?" I asked, a little more loudly than I intended.

"You know nooky wears both of us out," she whispered, putting a finger to her lips. "We have a hard climb today. You'll just have to wait until we get home."

My dream-self laid back and watched the wind play a noisy rhythm against the tent.

As I woke, the mists swirled in my painting, and the dot of firelight again gleamed out like a beacon from between the trees for a few seconds before it faded.

I hadn't really noticed if Patty had been wearing the ring in the restaurant. Would she wear it now that her lover was dead? I'm not that good at observing things. But in the dream, a round diamond was set in a bejeweled band, wide enough to carry the inscription. I shook my head. I'd never get to know.

Deciding I should go to work; I got dressed.

°

After taking care of some pressing business at work, I asked one of my employees, Nancy Demoors, if she knew much about Thatcher Ian Febbron. Nancy, a petite brunette with hazel eyes and tight corkscrew curls, is a talented novelist who ended up working for me after I'd promoted her first book a few times. Nancy is our hatchet person. You wouldn't think it to look at her, as she's 5' 4" with an angelic face. If I had to describe her in one word, it would be ebullient.

We'd met three years ago because she was local, and I'd advertised for someone who liked books to help the selection process of the books we promoted. At that time, we already had more submissions than we had room for in our daily newsletters. We didn't want to overwhelm our subscribers with too many choices, nor cheat our authors of the attention their advertisement deserved by drowning the readers with too many books.

As I had guessed, Nancy knew all about Thatcher Ian Febbron.

"Oh, yes, he is rather famous around here," Nancy said.

"For his paintings?" I asked.

"For that and for his mountain climbing," she replied. We were in her office. I had the single-story building designed so that every employee had a window wall view of Blue Mountain. There was a bird feeder outside high enough up in a thin tree that it was out of reach of the bears. A squirrel had climbed to it, and a Blue Jay was watching, waiting for the squirrel to leave.

"More famous for mountain climbing?" I asked. I've heard that his paintings go for quite a lot."

"He climbed K2," she said. "I suppose he might be more famous to mountain climbers as a climber. My Brad climbs a bit. There was an article about his K2 climb in the paper. He chose K2 because Everest has a queue you have to wait in to go to the top. It's so crowded people have died because they ran out of oxygen while waiting above 26,000 feet (7,924.8 m). And K2 is said to be more challenging anyway." She paused for a second. "There's a mountain named Annapurna that has a 40% climber death rate, but many believe K2 is deadlier. Thatcher was one of less than 200 that successfully climbed K2. But you are probably right about his being more famous as an artist. His paintings go for a bundle. I wish I had one."

"Maybe I'll get one for the office," I said. I didn't want to mention I already had one, just yet.

"You better hurry. Since he died, Febbron's paintings are selling like hotcakes," Nancy said.

She thought for a moment then gave me a questioning look. "You know there's a rumor his fall wasn't just an accident."

I looked at Nancy with surprise. "He was murdered?"

"It's just a rumor, and it might be that that is all it is. But he was supposed to be so good and so careful some people can't believe he died climbing." She paused for a second, thinking. "There's a guy in Missoula who climbed with him. He runs a little-used sporting equipment store downtown near the railroad tracks.

°

My office sat in the corner of the building. I went to my desk and grabbed the yellow pages. I found a number for what probably was the place on Alder Street and dialed the number.

The ringing stopped, and a deep voice said, "Second Time Sports. How may we help you?"

"Do you carry mountain climbing equipment?" I asked.

"Yes, we do have some," the man said.

"I'm new to climbing, and I don't know too much about it. Are you someone who knows much about climbing?" I asked.

"Yes," he said enthusiastically. "I'm a climber and the owner here. I also offer climbing lessons if that might be something you'd be interested in?"

"I might be," I said. I looked at my watch. It was going on 11 a.m. I'm out by Blue Mountain. If I swing by now, will you be there?"

"Sure, come on by," he said. "Mr.?"
"Frost, Kevin Frost," I said. "And you are?"
"Martin Teufel," he said.
"Well, Martin Teufel," I replied. I'm on my way."

o

o

It wasn't the store that made me ill at ease. The long and narrow corridor of it seemed crammed with almost every type of sports equipment. Bicycles stood bunched like scared cattle in the center between two isles. Snow skis and water skis crisscrossed between life jackets. Hockey masks, catcher's masks, and football helmets of various sizes hung high on the walls like game mounts. The place smelled of canvas and neoprene. There was even an unfolded hang glider suspended from the ceiling. Behind a low battered-looking oak desk sat a grizzled man about my age who stared up at me. I felt a shudder as I met his brown-eyed gaze. This was the man who had looked at me in my dream—both times with hostility. For a moment, I had to fight to keep my composure. 'This man doesn't know you at all,' I told myself. He was looking at me with what seemed amusement as if he were sizing me up. He stood.

"Mr. Frost," he said, extending his hand.

I stood frozen for a moment. Nancy's words came back to me. "There is a rumor his fall wasn't just an accident."

"Yes," I said, catching myself. "You must be Mr. Teufel?"

He led me to a display of new and used climbing equipment.

I stayed in the store for some time. By the time we were done, I had a small pile of equipment on the counter, from a new 60-meter climbing rope with carabiners built into either end to an almost new-looking Blue Ice Axe. It was not in my immediate plan to do snow mountain climbing, but the axe was cool looking and such a bargain I couldn't pass it up. I also had a climbing harness and a chalk bag, and chalk. What I didn't have was shoes. Martin told me it would be best to rent some at the climbing gym because you needed to climb with them to make sure you had a good fit.

I had a contract in front of me for ten climbing lessons, two of which, a morning and a late afternoon lesson, would begin tomorrow at the Boulder Family Climbing Center. The center is an indoor rock climbing gym where Martin was an instructor. Why had I signed up? I asked myself that question in the store as I plunged forward, buying gear as if climbing were something I seriously wanted to do.

I looked up from the contract into Martin Teufel's brown eyes. "You've never lost a student have you?" I asked. "I mean to a fall."

"No," Martin said. "We'll start with what is called bouldering. We'll do this in the gym. Basically, you'll start out free climbing, that's climbing without a rope, on a not-too-high indoor climbing wall. The floor is a padded landing, so you won't be hurt even if you do fall. After you've learned some basics, including the proper way to fall, I'll introduce you to what is called belaying on a much higher wall.

"In fact, the only student I ever lost decided she didn't like heights," Martin said.

I bent down to sign, and he added. "In the way of full disclosure, I should say I did lose one friend on a climbing expedition. He was Thatcher Ian Febbron."

"The famous painter?" I asked, feigning surprise.

"Yes, he was a painter, too." Martin continued. "But we in the climbing game thought of him as a mountaineer first. He actually climbed K2, considered by some to be the toughest mountain in the world."

"How did he die?" I asked.

"An unforeseeable accident," Martin said, with a concerned look that somehow came off to me as faked. "He got hit by a falling boulder that no one could see coming. There won't be any falling boulders in the gym. Most people who die make stupid mistakes, like not checking their equipment thoroughly. But Tif did everything right; he was just unlucky."

"But you are going to check my equipment?" I asked.

"I am going to teach you to check your own equipment, to make it far less likely that anything bad will happen to you," he said sternly.

I left shortly afterwards with a list of YouTube videos to watch on how to fall. Martin said he couldn't have a falling demonstrator lined up for our first lesson, and he didn't do the falls himself anymore because of cracked ribs. But it was essential for me to know from the start how to fall.

o

I had to return to the office. When I got there, an older-looking, green Land Rover Defender sat parked next to Holly Stein's neon-green VW bug.

Holly's mother, Karin Stein, was my office assistant and bookkeeper and the day before had been making up some checks for me to sign. I trusted Karin and would have given her permission to sign the checks for me. She refused. She said it was too easy for a bookkeeper to be tempted if said bookkeeper had the power to sign her employer's checks. So, she didn't sign checks, and for that, I trusted her even more.

As I walked in, Holly Stein, Karin's rail-thin, sixteen-year-old daughter who worked part-time as a receptionist, rose from the reception desk with the stack of checks I needed to sign in her hands. Her shoulder-length blonde hair framed her pretty, elf-like face. Karin complained that boys were already calling her too often for Karin's comfort.

"Thank you, Holly," I said.

The office was empty. Her mother often let the staff go a little early if everyone finished their work for the day. Hamil Warder, our computer geek, was often the last in the office, but, apparently, he had left too.

"Mr. Frost? "Holly began, somewhat timidly. "A woman came to see you a little while ago. Everyone else left for the day, and I didn't know what to do." She put her hands together and laced her fingers, a gesture I'd learned to associate with nervousness on her part. She'd done that during her initial interview with me.

"I let her wait in your office," she added nervously. "I hope that's alright?"

"That's fine, Holly," I said reassuringly. "You had to make a decision, and you did. You're a good receptionist."

"May I go now, sir?" Holly asked. She looked relieved.

"Sure," I said. "Just lock the door as you leave."

She nodded and began picking up her personal belongings.

I would have to talk to her about never letting people into my office, but I'd do it another time. There was no point in ruining her evening.

The truth was we didn't really need a receptionist. Not as a greeter. Though it was nice to have someone field phone calls, we didn't get much foot traffic in our business. I just feared the woman she had let in was a disgruntled author whose book we had turned down for a book promotion.

The last unhappy author, whose book had more grammatical errors and typos than I ever thought possible for a book, had had to be removed by the police.

As I walked to my office, I prepared myself for a difficult

encounter.

°

My breathing stopped, my heart fluttered, and I felt dizzy as a moment later Patty Ann Calloway rose from the visitor's chair in front of my desk to greet me.

"I hope you don't mind my coming here?" She asked.

For a moment, I was speechless. My heart was beating rapidly. There was, I realized, no reason for my reaction. I barely knew this woman. I'd only met her twice. And yet, I felt I was in the presence of someone whom I had strong if confusing feelings for.

I actually shook my head to make sure I wasn't dreaming.

"I don't mind," I said, holding out my hand.

Patty took it. Her grip was firm. She was wearing the perfume that smelled like lilacs again.

"I did not think I was going to see you again," I confessed.

Her eyes met mine. She had a strength I admired. "I didn't think I would see you again either," she said.

"But you're here," I said, lightly. I smiled.

She didn't return my smile. She studied me closely and asked, "May I see the painting? Is it here?"

"Sorry," I said. "It's at my home, in my bedroom." I felt tempted again to tell her that I had dreamt about her too. But I dismissed the idea.

She just looked at me.

"It's just five minutes away," I said. "I can go home and get it and bring it back if you want."

She studied me long enough to make a decision. "I can go with you," she said. "I'll follow you in my car."

°

As I guessed, the green Land Rover was Patty's. As she opened the door, she said over the hood, "You don't need to drive slow. I can keep up."

My home was literary minutes away. I had bought my expensive house between the Blackfoot River and Blue Mountain for tax purposes. In it, I had a home office I could use to run the business from if I had to.

I felt suddenly self-conscious as I turned into the open gate. My property is an 8-acre mini-ranch, and the driveway winds up a small hill through some partly open fields, dotted with copses of trees, to the two-story house, which is basically a mini-log-mansion with lots of glass.

I pulled my 2011 Prius that my late wife had picked out in front of the garage. Patty pulled up as I got out, realizing my car gave one impression and the house quite another.

"Wow," she said. "This is some house!"

"Yeah," I said. "Autumn and I got a little carried away."

"It's beautiful," she said.

"I can give you a tour," I said, "or would you just like to see the painting.

"Let's just do the painting," she said. Again her gaze was no-nonsense, and I thought a little cold.

o

I felt self-conscious, leading her to my bedroom. I often didn't make the bed and hadn't this morning. Taking the room in from the point of view of a visitor, I realized it was a mess.

"I'm sorry," I said. "I don't usually anticipate visitors to my bedroom."

Patty didn't reply. I pointed at the wall opposite the bed. As my eyes fell on the painting, my heart sank. I should have expected it. The red pinpoint of the fire was gone.

Patty looked the painting over quickly. "I don't see anything resembling a fire," she said pointedly. Truth be told, she sounded annoyed.

"It was there this morning," I said. "I probably wouldn't have even seen it from the bed except when I woke; it was almost glowing like a light."

Patty Calloway just stared at me.

"I took a photo," I said and scrambled to get my iPad which I'd left on the night table.

It took a while for the iPad to fire up. I felt Patty's eyes on me the whole time. I felt even more nervous because we were in my bedroom. When it finally started, I was fumble-fingered finding the photos.

But then it came up. And the fire was there in the photo. I walked over to her to show her, and she took a step back.

"Let me just take it?" she asked. She obviously didn't feel comfortable being too close to me.

I handed the iPad over. She studied it for a full minute.

"Do you have Photoshop?" she asked.

"At work," I said, "not on my iPad. And I took that this morning and the iPad has been here ever since. And I had no idea you'd be coming here today."

The look the beautiful young woman gave me was sad. She held the iPad out, handing it back. "I wish I could believe you," she said. She turned to leave.

"I have been having more dreams about what the people in my dreams called 'the climb.'"

Patty turned back, her eyes widened, but she didn't say anything. She just stood there for a moment then turned to go again.

"I've been dreaming about this climb," I said quickly. "As if I'm there. In our dream, I proposed to you. In front of our tent."

Patty turned, and her expression was angry. "Have you been talking to people about me?"

There was a flash of light as her hands moved, and I realized she was still wearing Tif's ring.

"No," I said. "I dreamt that the morning after Tif had given you the ring, you were trying to read the inscription in the dim light. So, he told you it said: 'You take me ever higher. All my love forever, Tif.' The ring looked like the one you are wearing. Is that the inscription inside?"

Patty Ann Calloway's face suddenly turned pale. "I don't know how you could know that." Then she seemed to be summoning her strength. "I think I'd better leave."

As she turned to go, I said, "No one told me that."

She was already walking out the bedroom door. I followed.

"In our tent, you couldn't read the inscription in the morning light. He suggested you go outside. You replied, 'Stark naked?' You were both whispering in your sleeping bags which were zipped together."

Patty stopped in her tracks. She stood still for a moment, then turned back. There were tears in her eyes.

"Please don't do this to me?" She cried. "He was everything to me."

With that, she hurried out the door. I heard her car start up and then the sound of her driving off.

DAY 7: SATURDAY

o

I awoke from a dream that started out with everyone congratulating us again in the morning on our engagement except for Martin Teufel, who said, "I gotta take a piss," and then walked off behind some boulders.

Patty didn't seem to notice or, perhaps she was ignoring him. I didn't seem to have much ability to choose what to pay attention to in my dream. I tried but discovered again; I couldn't say what I was thinking. It was the same as if I was in a movie and my lines had already been recorded.

We packed the tents, and then everyone donned their climbing equipment. Patty and I checked each other's harnesses.

We started out moving along fairly level ground. Patty hiked by me for the first part of the morning with a smile on her face, and I felt the warm glow of her company. We came to a spot where we had to walk single file. The trail followed a narrow ledge with a scree slide on one side and a steep drop on the other. Normally, I am terrified of heights. At age six, I tried to build a treehouse. The boards came loose, and I fell, splitting my forehead open. But in the dream, the steep drop at my side didn't bother me. I watched an eagle float along almost 100 yards below me. There had to be at least 9-football-field-lengths of air between the eagle and the ground. The sun in the brilliant blue sky felt warm on my face. I hadn't realized I had stopped until Patty poked me in the butt with a finger and said, "Move along kiddo."

I didn't want the hike to end. Finally, we came to a little open natural balcony—the trail changing to the thinnest of ledges clinging to an almost vertical rock wall.

There were small scrub pine here. Most of the guys put their packs down. I understood we'd be taking a rest.

Patty snuggled up to me.

The first hint of real tension in the party came when it was time to leave, and everyone was getting ready to rope up. Martin stood and made to go in front. This surprised me because I knew it was my turn.

"I think it's Tif's turn to lead," the tallest guy in the group, who I heard addressed as Peter, said.

"Oh, come on," Martin Teufel said. "What difference does it make?"

I'd come to understand that the climb, including the rest breaks, had been pretty much planned out ahead of time and that although Martin had done much of the planning, Tif was the group leader. This made it surprising that Martin had tried to take the lead.

Patty seemed to be staring at Martin. She looked annoyed.

"It's Tif's turn," the man I knew as Jessie, the youngest member of our group, said.

"Come on, Martin. We're burning daylight," the man I learned was John Bower said. He was the oldest member of the group.

Martin Teufel frowned but waved me to the lead.

I found myself moving out along a tiny ledge in the rock face. It was more of a crack than a ledge, but my toes had no trouble finding purchase on it.

Instead of terrifying me, the height seemed to thrill me. Small protrusions at about face height were large enough to crimp my fingertips around. In climbing terms, such handholds are called crimps. Using these crimps for my hands and the ledge for my toes, I worked my way along the ledge until I found a palm-sized crack ascending the wall.

o

o

I found myself reaching for one of the quickdraws attached to my harness with a cam on the end. A quickdraw is a strap of nylon with non-locking carabiners at both ends.

The cam I chose had three sets of bright yellow half-moons of aluminum at the top. It was the size cam I needed for the width of the crack we were following. When compressed, the cam's half-moons would contract like clock faces cut in half along a line from 12 to six. When released, they would spring back into 9 to 3 half-moons. In its wider position, the cam could be firmly locked into a crack. The team used cams because they are less damaging to the rock face than pitons, the pointed metal spikes with loops I had found in the closet in Tif's mini barn. The cams were also more easily removed to use again.

I set the yellow cam into the crack and released it. Then I pulled on it to make sure it was firmly set.

o

The team was connected by one long climbing rope. As lead climber, I was at the outgoing end of the rope, called the sharp end, with the rope attached to my harness. I pushed the rope into the quickdraw's free carabiner end.

Peter was below me, and as I moved upward, he fed out more rope. Now, because of the cam, I'd just placed, if I fell, Peter could stop my fall.

I pushed myself higher on the wall, looking for another place to set the next anchor.

o

As I came fully awake in my bed, the mists on the mountain were again moving. I watched them sleepily but then saw something that set my heart to pounding. Fear filled me, and my first thought was that it was a burglar out to rob me, perhaps to steal this very valuable painting. Then I took in the tall man with shoulder-length, dark, reddish-brown hair, a full-chin beard, broad shoulders, and bulging biceps standing to the left of my painting. The man did not move nor speak. He just stood there staring at me, dressed in a leather jacket, a blue-checked shirt, and jeans. And then I realized who it was. His shirt matched the one I'd dreamed of putting on in the tent. Somehow, even though he was across the room, his green eyes blazed into mine. I sensed not anger but a pleading in those eyes. Thatcher Ian Febbron vanished as I lifted my head from my pillow.

My heart was still beating wildly. The man standing by the painting had looked before he faded away, as solid as you or me.

I lay in bed, trying to make sense of the figure I had just seen. Why had Tif appeared to me? What did he want from me?

It occurred to me that I had not done any research on the accident itself. It was barely 7 a.m. I had time before the first of the two climbing lessons I had scheduled for the day to do some research.

Our office was usually closed over the weekend—far different from when Autumn and I first started the company and worked long hours every day of the week--so I had the place to myself.

Using a program called Devon Agent, I started a thorough search on many different search engines and internet sites for anything on Thatcher Ian Febbron. Unlike a Google or Bing search, Devon can be set to go into depths, probing PDFs and other documents. As my search started, I drove to a nearby restaurant for breakfast.

When I returned home, I found that Devon had found literally hundreds of references to Tif.

I discarded, for the moment, references to his paintings and his exhibitions.

I found about 26 articles about his climbing K2 and learned from an almost equal number of mentions; he had also been on a successful climb of Denali in Alaska.

There were multiple obituary listings in various newspapers; I would read them in good time. But what I was looking for was anything on the climb of the mountain in my painting and/or the accident that killed him. Finally, I hit pay dirt. The web page title was: 'Climbers to tackle Ungacongagru.' The date on the post was last year in July. That would have been just a month before Tif's last climb.

I opened up the page and discovered it wasn't a newspaper article but instead a YouTube video by a fellow who was an avid climber himself and posted videos about other climbers' efforts. The thumbnail was a photograph of the mountain in the painting that hung in my bedroom. I expanded the screen to full size and started the video.

After a little blurb by Walter Wessex, for his 'Ever Upward' channel, I came to a shot of the five men from my dream, Patty Calloway, and a man who was the image of the man I had awakened to see this morning standing in my bedroom.

Wessex was a short, wiry man with wild-looking brown hair. He smiled at the camera and then addressed Thatcher Ian

Febbron.

"So Tif," Wessex said, "This is your group for attacking Ungacongagru. Can you introduce us?"

"Sure, Walter," Tif said. His voice was deep and matched his broad shoulders and almost gymnast physique. "But I wouldn't say we plan on attacking Ungacongagru. You don't attack a mountain. You try to learn from it."

Wessex nodded.

"This," Tif said, indicating the tallest member of the group. The man had short curly blond hair and a hawk-like face. He stood a few inches taller than Tif, "is Peter Lambas. He's 25 and a physics Ph.D. candidate at Stanford. He has climbed most of the mountains in Washington state.

"Next is John Bower. He's the old man of the group at the old age of 36. He climbed with me on Denali."

Bower was the shortest of the group. He wore his short dark hair in a brush cut. I remember his smiling stubbled face from my dream. He seemed that most pleased when Patty mentioned the engagement.

"He's a professor of English at the University of Montana," Tif continued.

"Next," Tif said, "we have Jessie Bock…"

Bock was the youngest looking of the group. He had a mop of brown hair and steel blue eyes. He was just a bit taller than Bower. "He just graduated from the University of Wisconsin, Oshkosh, with a degree in Journalism. He will be chronicling our adventure. Jessie has written about numerous climbs in areas like Devil's Lake, Wisconsin. This will be his first 10,000-foot climb."

Tif moved to a dark-skinned, smooth-shaven man with jet-black, kinky hair and handsome features who stood slightly taller than Bower.

"Land Donahue, here, is not quite as old as John Bower. So, he's a little faster with things." Tif glanced over at Bower, who gave him the finger. "Which is good because he's an EMT in real life and our medic on this trip. I met him on K2. He is an accomplished climber."

Tif nodded to the one man whose entire name I knew. "Martin Teufel comes to us from Europe originally. Where, as a teenager, he honed his climbing skills on mountains like the Eiger.

"His parents moved to the United States when he was 19, where he took on Mount Saint Helens and Mount Rainier before his 21st birthday. He has been the major planner for this climb."

Tif smiled when he looked at Patty. "Patty Ann Calloway is a grade schoolteacher, an accomplished musician, and one of the best climbers in our group. I met her at a presentation she did on a climb up Kilimanjaro in Africa."

"Thank you, Tif," Wessex said, stepping forward. "So the question is, why Ungacongagru?"

"Well," Tif said, "It hasn't been climbed. Martin did the research and found that two groups attempted it in 1904 and then 1906. The leader of both groups, Alexander Thato, was an avid climber born in Kenya, Africa, who accompanied Hans Meyer on his 1889 summit of Kilimanjaro. It's rumored that before Kilimanjaro, he made the summit of Mount Kenya at age 19, 13 years before Sir Halford John Mackinder's 1899 'first' summit.

"Thato, as the first to discover Ungacongagru, was allowed to name it. Both his 1904 group and his 1906 Group failed to reach the summit. The first due to weather problems. A microburst blew so many trees down on the route to the base of the mountain; they couldn't get to the mountain.

"The second lost all six men to a fall off a cliff face. Faulty equipment was blamed for that.

"We'll be climbing next month, and we expect to have good climbing conditions in early August."

"Just how long does it take to plan a trip like this?" Wessex asked.

"Martin came up with the idea about a year ago, and, in fact, it will be a year this coming Thursday," Tif said. "He asked me to be group leader, and I contacted a number of climbing friends. And these are the guys who had the time and the inclination.

"By August 13th last year, with all of us working together, we came up with a schedule and a route to use in our ascent."

"How long will the ascent take you?" Wessex asked.

"We're planning on just five or six days to reach the summit," Tif answered "This isn't like a climb on a mountain like Denali where we would need weeks and a ton of supplies for the climb. The mountain is mostly snow-free in August, and the attraction is the technical rock climbing."

As Wessex wrapped up his video, I studied the group. Patty was smiling almost beatifically at Tif. I noticed Martin watching her with an intense expression on his face.

Thinking of Martin, I looked at my watch. I needed to leave then to make my morning appointment with him at the Boulder Family Climbing Center for my first instructions.

After I'd changed in the locker room, Martin Teufel was waiting for me in the main gym. The place was huge, with vertical and leaning walls covered in innumerable different-sized colored objects that climbed the walls in what seemed haphazard patterns.

I was just a few minutes late, and Martin looked peeved.

"Sorry," I said, walking up to him. "I thought this place was a few blocks East of here."

I had my climbing harness on, with my chalk bag attached.

He ignored my comment and reached for my harness. "Let's get this harness on correctly; then we'll rent you some shoes. As I told you in the store, you need to get the right fit."

As I tried on the second pair of shoes, Teufel said, "They can be a little tight, and definitely not too long. You are going to need your toes."

"Speaking of tight," I said, "this helmet you sold me is a little tight."

"Stop by the store, and we'll exchange it," Martin said.

I paid for the shoe rental and a Day Pass after signing a release saying I would not sue the climbing center if I incurred an injury.

"Okay," Martin said, "You are going to fall. You need to deal with it. Did you watch the videos I asked you to watch?"

"Yes, I did," I said.

He was looking me over. The videos covered not only falling techniques, but tips like removing phones, keys, things you could land on that could hurt you. I'd left everything in my locker.

Was Martin annoyed I'd been 4 minutes late or was he just not that friendly in general? I wouldn't say I liked his attitude, but I'd already paid him for my lessons, so threatening to quit if he didn't mellow out wouldn't help me.

An unsmiling Martin led me to a climbing wall that appeared to be 12 feet high. I saw a man and a woman race up a much higher wall further down in the gym, grabbing onto the colored climbing holds on the wall.

"People race up these?" I asked.

"Oh, yes," Martin said. "It may be another Olympic sport soon."

I had noticed that not all the walls were vertical. Some leaned outward before straightening, creating overhangs. There were even nooks and crannies. Attached everywhere on the walls were different colored, different sized shapes. They looked, for the most part, like the surface of some vanilla ice cream bowl that had been sprinkled with colorful sprinkles, gummy bears, sour snakes, and M&Ms.

The 12-foot wall in front of me was completely vertical, and its projections were of the larger sort.

Looking down at my feet, I realized that the floor here and throughout the climbing area was covered with thick blue padding.

Down the main corridor of the gym, a woman with wisps of blonde hair showing beneath a pink helmet set her foot waist-high on a tiny grey nob that looked like a seashell. I watched her jump upward, catching both hands atop a smooth red shape that resembled a female breast just above her head.

"This is the easiest climb in the gym," Martin said, indicating the wall we stood before, "It's rated a VB. The baby level." He pointed to an almost straight column of plastic inserts that I now saw looked to be two-inch deep, foot-long, imitation stones that protruded from the face of the wall. The way they were set resembled a sort of ladder.

"Why don't you put some chalk on your hands and try it?" Martin said. He was watching me now with a bemused expression. "Use the baby rungs and climb to the top."

I turned to the wall. It looked easy enough. I grabbed one of the ladder-rung stones just above my head, set the toe of my right foot on the lowest rung, and began climbing.

It seemed easy going, and I ascended rapidly until I found myself in a position where the next ladder-style rung was much farther to the right. My feet were a good five feet off the ground, and as I mentioned before, heights since age 6 were never my strong point.

I fished around with my right hand and found a tiny rock I could squeeze to get leverage to get my foot over to the far-right rung. But a second later, I realized I suddenly had nowhere to go. The next handhold was even further to the right and too far out of reach. If I let go with my right hand in the position I was in, I would fall. Realizing I needed to use my left hand to grab the rock, I moved back to where I had been. I slipped my left hand under my right arm, grabbed the tiny rock, and moved over. I could then grab the further away hold with my right hand.

There were a few more adaptations I had to make to put my hand on the top finally. I started back down, thinking I'd at least conquered this easy task.

"How did I do?" I asked Martin, feeling a tiny bit proud of myself when I reached the bottom.

Martin grinned. It was the closest thing to a smile I'd seen all day. "You did it wrong," he said. Then he began walking away.

"What do you mean I did it wrong?" I asked, deflated, as I chased after him.

He turned, and this time he had a genuine smile on his face. "First lesson in any climbing situation. Plan your climb before you go up. If you had taken a few minutes to study this easy ladder, you would have seen that you had to make changes to reach the top. You wouldn't have had to fumble around changing hands as you climbed. You would have known which hand to use."

What he said made sense.

"Come on back; I'll explain some of the hand and footholds on the climbing wall."

Before the lesson was over, I'd tried and knew the difference between slopers, something like the smooth breast-shaped thing I saw the jumping woman grab which you can only hold on to from below--or lean against, and crimps, the tiny rock I'd grabbed in my climb up the ladder-style rungs, which you hold with the tips of your fingers.

He had me try jugs—big ass pieces with large incut holds you can easily grab onto and pinches which I had to use my thumb to clamp onto, like squeezing a loaf of bread. I'd also learned the value of chalk. After a while, my hands had started to sweat, and without the chalk, they would have slipped off some of the holds.

Martin walked me out to my car after we'd showered and changed. He reminded me of our second lesson that evening and said goodbye. I did not like Martin. From my dream, I felt both dread and anger toward him. But I had to admit he was an excellent teacher.

o

o

I had some shopping to do so it was some time after saying goodbye to Martin when I got home.

To my surprise, I found Patty Ann Calloway's Land Rover in my driveway. Patty stood next to it, with an unreadable look on her face.

I got out of my car and stood. She didn't move. "Hi," I said. "I didn't expect to see you again. Have you been waiting long?"

"No," she said.

As I moved closer to her, I realized that she looked as if she was nervous. I had an image in my mind, because of the dreams I'd had of her, that she was a tough woman without any give at all. So, a nervous Patty Ann Calloway was not something I would have expected. "What can I do for you?" I asked.

For the moment, she just stood there without saying anything.

"Can I get you some coffee?" I asked. "Or maybe you'd like a real drink."

"I'd like a real drink," she said. She seemed to pull together a smile at that.

°

I put down two rock glasses on the coffee table in the living room, both rusty nails with ice. I sat on the white couch facing the wall-to-ceiling window looking out at Blue Mountain. Patty Ann sat in a lounge chair to my right. She looked at me as if slightly embarrassed, then picked her glass up and took a sip. I waited for her to speak.

She took another long swallow and looked at me with wide sad eyes. "I came partly to apologize," she said.

"You don't need to apologize to me," I said, although I had no idea what she'd have to apologize for.

She held her hand up. "I do. I thought you were trying to... Well, I thought you found the jeweler Tif bought the ring from and got the inscription to get into my head for some reason." She paused and rubbed her fingers together nervously.

"This isn't necessary," I said.

"It is to me," Patty said. "I was accused of something I didn't do in high school. No one believed me, and that still bothers me."

She hadn't actually accused me. But she hadn't believed me, and in a way, that had hurt.

"Anyway, I had to go to a jeweler in town to find out who sold Tif the ring," she continued.

"Turns out Tif got it in Vegas. I called the Vegas jeweler who sold it to him. The man in Las Vegas had heard what happened to Tif and was very sympathetic. I told him I had lost my ring in the same climb. I never actually wear jewelry on a climb, but he didn't know that. I said I was thinking of duplicating the ring with the same inscription, and could he do that for me. He said he'd had a fire in the office. He'd been robbed, and the robbers set fire to destroy the video surveillance. They destroyed his files, and he no longer had a complete description of the order. He remembered the ring, but apparently, he did so many inscriptions; he couldn't remember the exact wording of the inscription on my ring. So, he couldn't have given it to you.

"I had also thought someone on the climb had overheard us. But Tif was whispering when he said I should go outside the tent to check the ring. It was a bit windy at the time. I don't think anyone could have heard us whispering.

"So I don't understand how you could have found out about the inscription on the ring and what we said the morning after he gave it to me. No one knows what the inscription says, besides me, not even Martin. And he'd never tell you if he did know.

"Martin?" I asked. Trying not to let it show that my heart was pounding.

"Martin Teufel," she said. "He was on the climb with us. I met him in Russia in 2014. He was an alternate skier for Austria, and I was an alternate for the United States. I don't know how I would have gotten along without him. He's been there for me since Tif died."

"I do know Martin, by the way," I said.

"You do?" she asked.

"I had my first climbing lesson with him today," I said. "I wanted to learn more about climbing because of my dreams. He was recommended."

"That is just it," she said, "I just can't believe that you know about the ring and what we said from a dream. Someone on the climb must have overheard us and told you."

I could understand why she didn't believe me. "I assure you," I said, "I've spoken to no one about you and Tif on the mountain."

"You expect me to believe that this painting..." she trailed off. She looked at me for a moment. "Was there any writing on the back of the painting? A note inside?"

"Not that I noticed," I said. I remembered how uncomfortable she seemed in my bedroom. "I can get it if you'd like to look it over?"

"Yes, please," she said.

○

She examined the painting and the frame carefully. "I don't see anything," she said. She scratched at the nameplate with a fingernail. "I didn't know Tif added a plate. It was hanging in our house, and I just never noticed. Why didn't you take the paint off the plate?"

"I never got around to it," I said. "I didn't want to damage the frame. With the glass, all I had to do was remove it."

"Do you have the glass?" She asked.

"It's in the garage," I said. "But I doubt it will be much help. I have some acetone there. We can get that paint off the plate too."

○

In the garage, I found the glass that had been in the frame where I'd placed it and handed it carefully to Patty. She held it up to look at it.

"Let me open the garage door," I said. I opened the door, and she stepped over by it to peer at the painted-over glass in the sunlight.

While watching her, I saw a glint of light above us over the hillside going toward Blue Mountain. There was a parking lot there, and I thought for a moment that it was a reflection off a car. And a moment later, I saw it again and had the feeling that someone was watching us.

"I don't see anything on the glass," Patty said. "You said you have something to take the paint off the nameplate?"

"Yes, I have acetone," I said.

I got the can and a rag and dripped some of the acetone onto the rag. "I don't want to get this stuff on the frame; it will probably take the varnish off easier than the paint on the plate.

Even using acetone, I had to rub quite a bit to get the long dried paint off the nameplate. Patty stood close to me, and I could almost feel her presence. Every once in a while, I looked out the garage door. I didn't see the flash of light again. But I still had the uneasy feeling we were being watched.

Finally, the words on the plate were readable. I stood and held the frame out to Patty so that she could read it.

°

--- Ungacongagru, August 13, 2019 —

°

"See, it's just a name and a date," I said.

I looked up to see Patty staring in horror at the label.

"Are you okay?" I asked.

She stepped back from the painting and me and stared at the small nameplate. "Why would he put that date on it? He finished the painting months before. I guess there were so many paintings on our walls I didn't notice it. Now I wish I had."

She looked at me. "I wanted you to be lying. I wanted you to have heard what that inscription said from someone on the climb. Or that the inscription on the ring was on the back of the painting or the frame." She looked at me intently for a long moment. "Do you dream about the climb every night?"

"No," I said. "Only when I'm in the room with the painting. When I went to Helena to see Tim, I stayed there and didn't dream about the climb at all."

Tears rolled from her eyes. "I don't know how this could be happening. I want you to be lying, and you are somehow dreaming about Tif and me; you're dreaming about things that are personal. Would you sell me the painting back?"

"Are you sure you want it?" I asked. "Wouldn't it remind you of what happened?"

"I want to buy it to destroy it," she said.

I thought for a moment. "I'll give it to you, but not just yet. I know you don't want to believe it, but I think Tif wanted me to have this painting. Was Tif in the lead on the first part of the climb the day he died?"

"You're saying you dreamed that?" she asked.

"Yes," I said.

"Someone could have told you that too," she said.

"I also dreamt about Martin giving me hateful looks."

She frowned and shook her head. "Martin isn't like that; he just doesn't smile much."

"I know you don't believe me," I said. "But I saw Tif's ghost this morning in my bedroom when I woke up. I think he wants me to see what happened to him. When I've done that you can have the painting. You don't need to buy it."

Patty's eyes filled with tears again, and she looked away. When she looked up again, she said, "I had a dream this morning about that very day; it was almost exactly as I remember it. It started out that I was with Tif. But then Tif, who was the lead climber at first, wasn't Tif at all. It was you."

She hesitated and then added, "And when I woke, Tif was in my room, standing near the bed, smiling at me. 'You need to talk to Kevin,' he said and then vanished.

I knew then that she was finally accepting, albeit reluctantly, that something otherworldly was going on.

"How far in advance did you plan this climb?" I asked after she calmed down.

"Over a year," she said, as she wiped tears away. "It was going to be less than a two-week climb to the summit and back. But Tif always liked to plan out things as early as possible." She paused for a moment collecting herself. "I suppose it might have been the date he planned on reaching the summit."

"You can predict how long it will take? Climbing a mountain, that is?" I asked.

"Yes, if you have everything planned out," she said. "Tif actually chartered a small plane that took photos based on his instructions, then had the photos emailed to him. He mapped the route and camps for each day. He sent everyone planning to be on the climb a newsletter with photos and possible routes. Tif had gotten everyone to contribute, so they felt like they'd had as much of a part as he did."

"Did anyone ever challenge Tif on his route?" I asked.

"No one really challenged him, in the sense of saying this isn't a good idea. Martin, who actually suggested the climb in the first place, did make one suggestion about the final climbs, which were the only technical climbs. We were doing the easiest one of those when Tif had his accident."

I didn't know what to say, so for a while, I said nothing. Then I broke the silence. "I'm a little scared. I wonder if this means we're going to be dreaming about the accident soon?"

"I don't know," she said.

We promised to keep each other up to date on our dreams. All too soon, Patty walked out the open garage door, got into her car, and drove off.

I watched her go wishing she could have stayed longer. Then, I remembered the flashes of light and scanned the hillside above me. I saw no one. Could whoever it was, be hiding in the trees that abutted my property? I still couldn't shake the feeling that I was being watched. I glance toward the trees casually but saw nothing suspicious.

I thought for a moment of hiking up the hill to the Blue Mountain parking lot above me. The public parking lot some distance above my home was the one used by the Frisbee golfers. I would often see their discs sailing through the air. Instead, I went back inside the house.

Within minutes, I had a briefcase in my hands and walked casually out to my car. I got in and drove at a normal speed down the driveway. As soon as I was too far away to be seen by any person watching from the trees, I sped up. I broke the speed limit, but police patrols in the area were few. It took me less than 5 minutes after leaving my driveway to get within sight of the parking lot.

No sooner had I pulled over when I saw a familiar figure appear rounding the top of the hillside from the direction of the trees bordering my property. A breeze blew his hair and rustled his shirt. A pair of binoculars hung from around his neck. Martin Teufel walked to a blue Land Rover and opened the door.

I immediately backed up and swung around. I drove off, not wanting Martin to see that I had seen him. Martin had no reason to be following me. That meant he had to be following Patty. In fact, it occurred to me why he had scheduled a break between our lessons; so that he could check up on Patty. Mixed emotions went through me. Anger, fear, and a very strong suspicion that he had, in fact, killed Thatcher Ian Febbron.

o

By the time of my second lesson of the day with Martin, I was torn over whether to call Patty Calloway and tell her what I'd seen. There was a massive problem, however. She'd known Martin a long time and trusted him. She barely knew me. I realized that even though I had only known her for a short time, I already had feelings for her. I knew I was probably infatuated, and my feelings were unrealistic. But even if my feelings were fantasies based on my dreams, I could not stand by and not do anything about Martin Teufel stalking her. I just knew in my heart that she was in danger.

I drove to the rock climbing center, intending to confront Martin. The scents of muscle rub and chalk seemed even stronger as I walked from the locker room to the gym. But I saw no sign of Martin. A muscular young woman with a long dark ponytail, a round face, and bright blue eyes approached me.

"Hi," she said with a smile. "I'm Jeanette Brown. Martin asked me to be your instructor for this lesson."

"He isn't here?" I asked; I must have sounded angry.

Jeanette looked a bit ruffled for only a second. She did look like she might be strong enough to take me in a fight.

"This is perfectly normal, and I'm highly qualified," she said evenly. "It's just that Martin really doesn't do the falling segment. Although he might stop in later."

I glanced around, thinking I might see Martin coming in. There was no sign of him.

"Falling?" I asked.

"How to fall," she said. "I was a gymnast, and I'm pretty good at this stuff. Martin says he's too old for it."

"So you're going to teach me this just in case I fall sometime?" I asked with a smile.

"Oh," she said, "if you climb, sooner or later, you are going to fall. This is about showing you how to do it."

I had watched the videos Martin had asked me to watch on falling. I would not have wanted to fall after only watching videos about it.

Jeanette led me to an area of the climbing gym studded with good-sized colored handholds on an overhanging wall. The highest point was about 10 feet off the floor.

"Now you can see here on the floor some portable pads," Jeanette said. "If sometime you're outdoors 'bouldering'—that's what climbing rocks is called—you might want to put down crash pads like these."

She picked up two blue pads about 6' x 6' that resembled the ones I'd used in gym class in high school to do tumbling exercises. She placed the pads beneath the center of the overhanging wall, one next to the other. "Now, here, these aren't that important. The floor itself is padded. It's one of the reasons why you have to wear clean shoes.

"If you were outside, you might be climbing an actual boulder, and I think Martin will eventually have you doing that. In such a climb, you might have more pads spread around the landing area. But first, you have to know how to fall. And I'm going to be showing you how."

She moved over the wall and placed her hands on two holds above her head. She then placed one foot on the lowest hold near the padded floor and then the other foot on a hold about two feet above the first.

"Now, I'm using my hands and the pressure I'm exerting on the footholds to keep myself--somewhat upside down--on the wall," she said. She climbed about three feet higher and then stopped. "Now watch what I do as I fall." With that, she let go. She fell on her back with her legs lifted.

Then it was my turn. I climbed only four feet up the overhanging wall. It wasn't too hard to let go. Finally, I was falling. I hit the mat with a woof. I fell as Jeanette had shown me on my back with my legs lifted. It knocked some of the air out of me, but I was okay.

In subsequent lessons, I learned to roll as I fell when my side was facing the floor so that I did not land on either arm but instead landed on my side.

On my last fall, I hung upside down at the top of the wall for the highest fall of my day. Directly below me, Jeanette had piled the two extra pads, one on top of the other. All of my previous practice falls had been from heights of no more than three and a half to four and a half feet. Now, at the very top of the climbing wall, I looked down and froze in fear—long seconds ticked by. My hands at first refused to release my grip on the two blue, jug-sized holds I clutched desperately with sweating, chalk-covered hands. And my feet seemed to want to press forever on the two brown protrusions, the tension on which kept me in place. Just before I forced myself to let go, a disturbing thought came to me. Martin had reminded me of my lesson but hadn't actually said he'd be here. What if, after seeing Patty at my house, he had gone to confront Patty?

I let go. Almost instantly, I hit the pads hard enough to force the air from my lungs.

Despite the extra pads, I felt a bit sore when I said goodbye to Jeanette.

o

I drove home. I realized I hadn't actually seen him watching us. I had no actual proof to offer Patty. Martin's being at the Frisbee park could be explained as a coincidence. What I needed to do was learn as much as I could about him. I needed to talk to some of the other members on the fatal climb. But how would I get them to talk to me?

An idea soon hit me. I made a side trip and bought a throwaway cell phone.

o

I reached Land Donahue first, only because he was home with a sprained ankle. When he picked up the phone, he thought I was someone else.

"Yeah, I know I'm stupid," a gravelly voice said, "how was I to know I'd trip while playing catch with the dog?"

"Land Donahue, I believe you're thinking I'm someone else," I said. "I'm calling from Missoula, and I'm sorry for your injury."

"Missoula," he said, concern suddenly in his voice. "Is she okay?"

"As far as I know, Ms. Calloway is fine at the moment. I saw her this morning," I said. "If that's who you mean?"

"Good," he said. "Yes, that is who I meant. Who are you?"

"My name is Steven Bauilding. I'm a therapist in Missoula, and I am calling with Ms. Calloway's permission," I said. Bauilding was a real person and a psychologist but totally unreachable as he was out of the country. I don't know if he would have approved of what I was doing, but it's easier to ask forgiveness than permission. "This call is about my treatment of Ms. Calloway, which I cannot discuss in-depth," I continued, "but can say it's similar to PTSD.

"This is about what happened to Tif on the climb?" he asked.

"Yes," I said. "Miss Calloway is having trouble remembering what happened on the climb, and we decided to see if I could find some of the other team members who might remember it."

There was a pause, and Donahue sighed. "I'd be happy to help. Though I don't know how much help I can be."

"Anything you can tell me would be greatly appreciated," I said. "And kept confidential."

"Well," Donahue began. "There were seven of us all together. Patty was the lead climber when the accident happened. Are you a climber?"

"No," I said. "I'd appreciate you explaining as much as possible."

"Patty was leading the group of us up the steepest part of the mountain. Peter Lambas was behind her, belaying her. That is, he was minding the rope attached to her. She was setting cams, removable protection, as she climbed. If she started to fall, Peter, being the strongest and heaviest member of the group, would stop her fall by securing the rope.

"John Bower, he was the oldest member of the group, was next on the rope after Peter. He was followed by Jessie Bock, who was relatively new. I was next on the rope, and Martin Teufel was behind me. Tif was the last in line when the accident happened. It was his job to get the cams out."

"I had thought," I said, "that Tif was leading that day?"

"Tif was in the first spot that morning. But we switched places after a break. Patty and Tif had gotten engaged the night before, and he wanted Patty to have a chance to lead," Land said. "She didn't even know something had happened to Tif at first."

"What exactly did happen to Tif?" I asked.

"Mountain climbing is dangerous for many reasons.", Land said. "Tif was on his way up when a piece of ledge came loose. It hit him on the head. Broke his nose, knocked out some teeth, and put him in a coma."

"There was nothing suspicious about the accident?" I asked.

Land hesitated. "I couldn't believe it. Tif was the most careful climber in the group. But you do get some falling rock on almost every climb."

"How does Tif being a careful climber, figure in to your not believing what happened to him?" I asked.

There was a silence on the other end of the line.

"You still there?" I asked.

"How is this going to help Patty?" Land asked.

"She needs to come to terms with what happened," I said. "How did she come to learn what happened?"

"Apparently, when he got hit on the head, Tif fell. Martin Teufel called, "Falling," which is what one does when someone falls. Tif did not fall far, only a few feet. He ended up hanging unconscious at the end of the rope, which was attached to all the rest of us. Luckily, the rest of us were on a rest and all attached to an anchor. Otherwise, had we been on a steep wall and just roped together, we might all have been pulled off the mountain.

"Martin climbed down to Tif and found him unresponsive. We had a heck of a time getting him down and out of there."

I had thought out what I wanted to ask next. "Based on the trauma that Ms. Calloway is experiencing, is there, was there, anything unusual in the way the accident happened?"

Another silence on the other end of the line lasted so long I thought Land had hung up on me.

Finally, the man spoke, "Just that Tif was extremely careful. I still have a hard time believing that that happened to him."

I thought we were done and was about to thank him and say goodbye when he added, "I went by the rock that fell on him. It looked stable on the shelf it fell from. I still can't imagine it falling.

"And I think that could be Patty Calloway's problem. We were zig-zagging up the mountain face following a crack. Tif had to be there in the spot where the rock fell at the exact time it fell. A second earlier, and it would have bounced on past him. A second later, and it would have just gone by him.

"Him getting hit by that rock was just the worst luck ever."

°

That evening after many unsuccessful attempts to contact Lambas, Bower, and Bock, I had a hard time falling asleep.

Eventually, I did.

DAY 8: SUNDAY

I awoke from a new dream in a sweat. The sheet on top of me and the sheet below me were cold and wet. I looked at the painting, and this time, for the first time, the mists were still.

In the dream, I kissed Patty just before she led the way for the day's climb. As I broke the kiss, I caught the expression on Martin Teufel's face. It could only be described as a look of hatred.

A short time later, Martin and I were on a talus slope heading toward a wall. The others were ahead of us, already climbing the wall. I knew they were following a crack that I could not see from where I was. I was watching Martin, who was ahead of me. The team had roped up at 25 feet apart. I was keeping an eye on him because I had an uneasy feeling. He reached the wall and began climbing along the crack.

I reached the crack soon after Martin and began climbing. My job was to remove the cams that Patty had set as lead climber. The crack zigged and zagged up the mountain. Its opening was a forearm wide, and as it had lots of hand and footholds, it was a relatively easy part of the climb. The challenging part of Ungacongagru was near the summit. It was there that Thato and his crew had fallen.

When I came to one spot where the crack switched from zig to zag, I could see Martin above me and Land Donahue climbing above him. I knew the rest of the team had reached the ledge where we would all anchor for a rest break. Land was just moving out of sight onto that ledge when I saw him. I then zagged to my left, and an outcrop of rock directly above me temporarily blocked my view. I had to linger at the switch spot for a moment to take out a cam that Patty had put in there as protection.

Having removed the cam, I moved up along the next zig. When I had moved far enough to be out from the under the outcrop, I saw Martin. He was on what looked like a dugout ledge directly above me. To my surprise, his safety rope was far to my right. He had obviously detached himself from the rope and had free climbed along the ledge to the spot where he sat now.

As the other members on the team were anchored on the ledge above, from their position Martin and I were both out of sight.

He had one leg wedged under the overhang of the dugout. His other leg pressed against a long flat rock sitting on the ledge. With a shove, he pushed the rock off the ledge. I tried to move, but for that instant, I was frozen.

Martin cried, "Falling!"

The rock came at my face. As It hit me, I fell backward, and then all I saw was darkness.

Some moments later, I found myself hovering out away from the cliff face. I was looking down on Thatcher Ian Febbron's limp body as it swung in the breeze.

I looked up and saw Martin Teufel, already hooked back to the safety rope, looking up and calling out to the other team members.

I rolled out of bed and vomited into my wastebasket.

Martin Teufel had murdered Thatcher Ian Febbron. And now I knew exactly how he had done it. His motive, I knew in my heart, was jealousy. He wanted Patty Calloway. He had met her first, and Tif had snatched her away from him.

I was never the sort of man who believed that a woman belonged to me simply because I wanted her. If, while I was dating my late wife, she had decided she wanted to be with someone else, I would have let her go. Love is letting the person you love find happiness, even if it is not with you.

I was awash with emotions. Martin had killed Tif to get Patty for himself. The question was: How long would he wait until he tried to force himself on her? He'd been following her the other day when she'd come to my house.

Before I fully understood what I was doing, I got myself dressed, got in my car, and was driving toward Patty Calloway's home.

o

There was a white picket fence in front of the red house with green and white trim that was barely a mile away from my own home. Hedges surrounded a front porch hung with hanging plants.

I had no idea what I would say to her when I climbed the front steps and pressed the doorbell.

I realized I was totally unaware of the time when the door opened, and a very surprised Patty Ann Calloway stood staring at me in the open doorway. She was wearing blue pajamas that accented her eyes. A blue bathrobe of the same shade hung on her shoulders.

She looked at me and then down at her wristwatch. "You're up early. Did you come to take me to church?"

"Would you want me to take you to church?" I asked.

She looked at her watch again. "If we hurry, we can make the 8 o'clock service," she said. "You can tell me why you came over on the way. Do you mind waiting out here? The place is a mess."

"I'm good," I said.

It didn't take long before she came out in a flowered dress and a blue shawl. "We'll take your car? Okay?"

I led her to the car. She looked surprised when I opened the door for her.

"What church?" I asked once we were both in the car. "St. Philips," she said, indicated the Catholic Church just a few blocks away.

"I...," started, but she interrupted me.

"Can we talk after Mass?" she asked.

"Okay," I said. I was raised Catholic, and I'd married Autumn in a Catholic Church in West Virginia, where she was from. We'd both attended St. Phillips before she died.

I had no idea why Patty wanted to go to Mass with me. I wouldn't have been surprised if she had just told me to leave when I showed up at her door at 7:25 in the morning.

Father O'Locklan, who had been Autumn's and my parish priest, apparently had retired. So, after the service, I didn't have to field any questions about not attending church recently when we met the new priest at the door. Father Thomas seemed to know Patty. They chatted.

It gave me a bit more time to figure out the best way to tell Patty about my dream of how Tif was murdered. I was so nervous my hands were sweating.

"How did you know I'd be willing to go to church with you?" I asked after we'd said goodbye to Father Thomas.

Patty didn't answer right away. She was looking in all directions as if searching for something.

"You have a St. Philip's sticker on your rear bumper," she said.

I laughed. "I forgot Autumn put that there."

"Your late wife?" Patty asked.

I nodded.

"Again, I am sorry for your loss," she said.

"And again, I'm sorry for yours." So many people said that to me that it usually didn't register anymore. But I could tell Patty was feeling a similar pain when she said it. "I never know how to respond to condolences," I added after a moment. "Autumn and I had two wonderful years together. In some ways, she's still with me."

"I can still feel Thatch with me, too," Patty said. She put her hand on my arm. "I had a dream about Tif"s accident. Did you dream about it too?"

"Yes," I said. "It's why I came."

"Can we talk about some other time?" Patty said. Tears appeared. "Some other day, actually. I'm not up to talking about it today."

I nodded. I tried to think of something to say.

"How did you meet Thatcher?" I asked. "If you don't mind me asking."

"In a bar," she said with a laugh. "He was a bit drunk, and with a group of his friends. Somehow, we just started talking. We talked for a long time, and then I had to go, but he asked me if I'd be back the next night. I said I would.

"He'd told me he was a painter who climbed mountains, so I looked him up. I thought his paintings were beautiful.

"He was a famous climber already as well. I went back to the bar the next night, and he didn't remember me at all."

"He didn't remember you?" I asked, disbelieving.

"No," she said. "It was embarrassing. Luckily, his friends remembered me. Thatch felt bad, and the next day he invited me to his studio. Most of his paintings were of mountains. I told him I'd done some climbing with Martin Teufel. Tif actually had heard of Martin."

"You mentioned you and Martin were both skiers. But you were also both climbers?" I asked.

"Martin was an accomplished climber. I'd never tried it. He took me climbing on our first date. I enjoyed it and got hooked," she said.

"You weren't dating Martin when you met Tif?" I asked.

"No," she said. "Martin was still asking me out, but I'd stopped accepting. I just didn't have any romantic feelings for Martin. I think because I stopped accepting his invitations, he finally got the message. But I still liked him as a friend."

She wasn't ready to talk about our dreams, but it didn't mean I couldn't mention what I knew about Martin.

I hesitated to say what I said next, "Martin Teufel was following you yesterday when you came to my house."

She seemed to freeze and stared at me, her expression unreadable.

"I noticed a flash of light when we were standing outside my house," I explained. "I suspected we were being watched. After you left, I drove up to the parking lot above my house and saw Martin walking to his car. Has he been bothering you?"

"No, not at all," she said, flustered. "Since Tif died, Martin has been there for me."

She looked at me for a long time then turned away. "I have felt someone watching me off and on for the past week," she said.

"So, it was most likely Martin," I said.

"No," she said. "In fact, if you did see Martin, he was probably trying to find out who is stalking me. He has been my best friend since Tif died. I don't know if I could have gotten through Tif's long stay in the hospital, and then his death without Martin. He even took care of all the arrangements for the funeral. I told him about having feelings I'm being watched, and I wouldn't be surprised if he were trying to find out who it was."

She paused for a moment. "I know I should feel guilty about letting Martin do things for me like this. I know he still has feelings for me. And I love him, but not in the way he'd like me to."

I realized right then that if I told her my dream about Martin killing Tif, she probably wouldn't believe me. She, obviously, thought Martin was a saint.

"So why did you come by this morning?" Patty asked.

"To tell you I had a dream, to see if you'd had one, and to tell you that I thought someone was watching you," I said.

"And you're sure they weren't watching you?" she asked.

"I'm not that interesting," I said.

"Well, thank you for not insisting we talk about our dreams. And forwarning me that someone is following me," she said and then added, "I think I'd like to walk home. It's not far. Thank you for coming to tell me and taking me to church."

"You're welcome," I said.

As she walked away, I wanted to go after her. But what good would that do? I realized if I went to the cops and told them Martin Teufel murdered Tif, they'd ask how I knew. When I told them I'd dreamt it, they'd throw me out or into a nuthouse.

As I drove home, I passed Patty. She waved and smiled.

o

As it was Sunday, I did not have a lesson with Martin, but the climbing gym was open, and I went there that afternoon. The hand and footholds were smaller on the more challenging climbing wall I worked on. I fell a few times and was glad of the falling instructions I'd gotten.

I went home exhausted. I wondered if I'd dream that night and thought that if I didn't, maybe I should just drop the whole thing. Patty might never believe me and might grow to hate me if I kept trying to convince her that Martin killed Tif. Patty and Martin Teufel could just go on with their lives. Even if Martin Teufel had murdered Tif, there was no way I could prove it nor do anything about it.

I almost resolved to do that. But then the idea of not seeing Patty again left me feeling an emptiness I hadn't experienced since Autumn died.

DAY 9: MONDAY

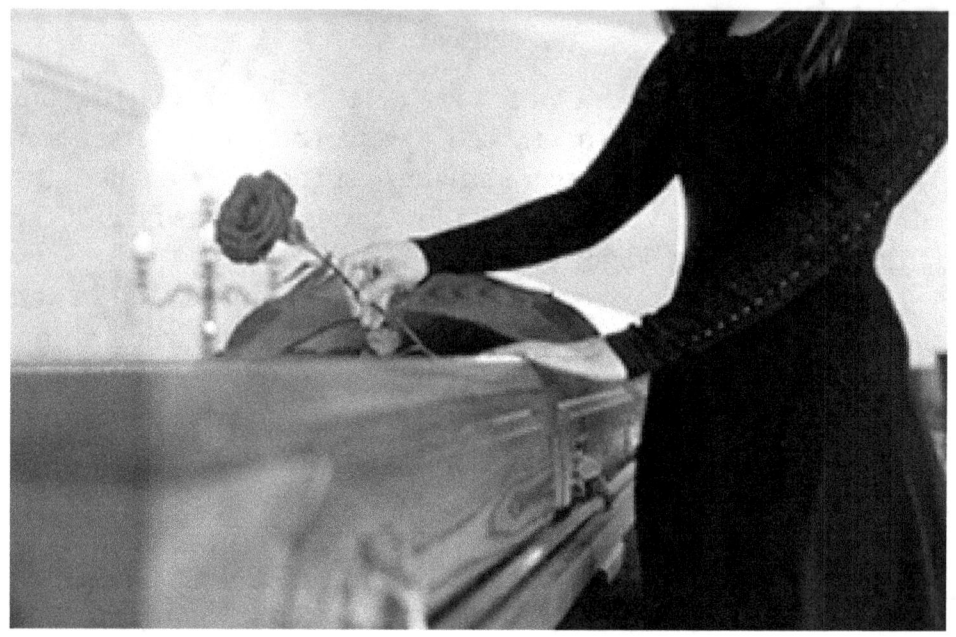

In a bright room that smelled like flowers, the body of Thatcher Ian Febbron rested in an oak coffin. The man I'd seen standing in my room by his own painting lay still and unreal-looking on a light satin pillow. Makeup seemed caked on the skin of his face. They'd done a good job of hiding his injuries.

Dressed in a suit, he held a small climbing cam in his right hand and a paintbrush in his left. Both hands rested over his heart. To the left of the coffin on a pedestal was a watercolor self-portrait of the man. In the painting, Tif was scaling a stone wall, facing upward at a slight overhang. Far below, tiny trees loomed carpet-like.

In the dream, I was hovering in the room. Patty walked in wearing a black dress. She had a red rose with her. Placing the rose in the coffin, she then knelt by Tif's side. Time passed slowly. When she rose, there were tears in her eyes. Finally, she bent down and kissed Tif on the forehead. As she turned away, Martin Teufel appeared and led her away.

However, as I watched this, I assume through Tif's spirit, I found myself focusing on Martin Teufel's possessive hand on Patty Calloway's arm. I felt a tremendous emotion which I assumed was anger. I felt myself twitching as if trying to move but unable to. And a thought came to me, a question really. How did Martin arrange for that accident to happen?

As I opened my eyes, the mists on the mountain painting were moving. It seemed as if they were more agitated now than they had been before. By the time they calmed to a still painting, I had a plan.

I had no idea how to find out whether Martin Teufel had gone to the mountain ahead of time to arrange the accident. But my tech guy Hamil Warder would probably know.

°

Hamil, who had been named after Mark Hamil of Star Wars fame, was at his desk when I arrived. Tall to the point of being a giant at 6' 5", his work desk almost looked like one from a first-grade class. I'd offered to get him a more comfortable one designed for big men, but he'd declined. His clean-shaven face, beneath a shock of black hair that always looked like he combed it in a windstorm, scowled down at a computer screen.

"Hey, boss!" He said with a smile.

"I have a special job for you. You'll have to do it after hours if you agree," I said.

"What's the job?" He asked.

"This is off the company books, so you'll be paid directly by me for doing it," I said.

Hamil nodded.

I explained what I wanted and said it was no problem if he couldn't or didn't feel comfortable with the job, as I could always hire a private investigator.

"You don't need a private investigator for that," he said. "I can do it myself."

"Good," I said. I was walking away and then turned back. I would go nuts waiting until tomorrow to learn what Hamil found out.

"On second thought, I need this as soon as possible," I said. "How about you work on this today, here? And get your regular work done tonight. I'll give you overtime for your work tonight as well as separate pay for the job itself.

Hamil looked like he wanted to ask a question but thought better of it. I didn't ask if he had plans. He usually stayed late in the office most nights, but I should not have presumed.

"I'll get on it right away," he said.

I barely got any work done myself that morning, waiting on Hamil's results.

°

Just after one thirty, Hamil, who'd worked through lunch, walked into my office and put a folder of printouts on my desk. "I think that's as much as we can get," he said.

According to the video I'd watched, the route for the climb itself had already been planned. The date of the interview was August 8th, a year before the actual climb. If Martin Teufel had gone to the mountain to set up the accident, he had to have traveled to the mountain sometime after that date.

The paperwork in the folder showed that Martin Teufel had booked a flight to Calgary in Alberta. He had then taken an airbus from Calgary to the Stoney Nakoda Resort, which was close enough to the base of Ungacongagru that the mountain could have been his destination. He had stayed one night at the resort and then taken off the next day. The problem was: There were many mountains he could have visited.

Hamil had added a note that the expedition that Tif led had flown to Calgary and then air-bussed to Canmore airport, which was even closer to Ungacongagru.

Another sheet indicated that Teufel had picked up climbing equipment in Calgary, which he had ordered ahead of time.

A rental agreement for a Jeep was in the papers that he picked up at the resort. But there was no information on where he intended to take the Jeep. But Hamil had been able to access the mileage on the vehicle when he returned it. Martin had driven far enough that he could have gone as close to Ungacongagru as needed to make a climb.

I pushed the folder away from me on my desk and looked out the window. As far as evidence that Martin had gone to Ungacongagru to set up Tif's murder, I had nothing. I took stock of what I did have.

Hamil had provided some additional research. Ungacongagru was only a 10,000-foot peak. The only reason it was attractive to climbers was that the last pitches that reached the peak were technical climbs that had never been successfully attempted before. Tif's group never made it to the problematic last parts of the climb. Tif was hit with the falling rock on a relatively easy pitch. The climb to where the accident occurred was something that Martin Teufel could have done easily on his own.

But there was a world of missing evidence between could do and did do.

I looked at my watch. I had about an hour before my late afternoon lesson with Martin Teufel. He had texted me that I should bring my harness as we'd be doing top roping that afternoon. Top roping meant I would be climbing the wall with a rope secured above me, tied to my harness. The rope would stop my fall if I fell. I had put my harness in the car that morning.

Not knowing what else to do, I decided to try the other climbers again.

With the burner I had purchased for the task, I dialed Peter Lambas's number first.

There was no answer after a dozen rings. A message came on

saying the mailbox was full.

I dialed John Bower's number.

"Yes?" A throaty voice answered.

"John Bower?" I asked, probably sounding surprised. When he said yes, I went into my spiel about being Patty Calloway's therapist. I must not have sounded as convincing as I had been with Land Donahue.

"How do I know you're her therapist?" Bower demanded.

"I guess you'll have to take my word for it," I replied, trying to sound jovial.

"Well, the thing is this," Bower said. "I'm not sure if I want to help Calloway. Tif was my best friend. We'd climbed Denali together. So, I wasn't pleased that this woman distracted Tif on his last climb. He only did the climb, which was supposed to be an easy one, so he could ask her to marry him on a 10,000-foot climb."

"You're saying that Tif's accident was Patty Ann's fault?" I asked.

"Not directly," Bower said. "But when you're climbing, you have to be focused. Tif wasn't as focused as he should have been."

For a moment, I didn't know what to say. Then an idea came to me. "Could you just tell me a little about what happened? I understand that Martin Teufel made a trip to Canada after the climbing plans were made to check out the route personally. So, Tif's accident had to be a surprise?"

There was a long silence on the other end of the line. Finally, Bower spoke. "I don't know anything about Teufel checking out the route. That's the first time I ever heard that.

"And I don't see how that information could possibly help Patty Calloway. If Teufel went, and if he told Tif the route was good, the idea the climb should have been safe would just make her feel worse."

"You are saying that Martin Teufel could have made the climb by himself ahead of time?"

Again there was silence on the other end of the line. "Most of it, yes. But what are you getting at?"

"Would Martin Teufel have had reason to want to hurt Tif

during the climb?" I asked.

"Shit," Bower said. I could sense his emotion.

I waited silently, hoping he wouldn't hang up.

"You know for a fact that he actually went up there ahead of our climb?" Bower asked.

"Let me ask this first. Would Teufel have been able to reach the mountain if he flew to the Indian Casino instead of Canmore?" I asked.

"Easily," Bower replied.

"He stayed one night at the resort and then vanished for a week," I said. "I've seen the paperwork."

"Why would Patty Calloway have the paperwork?" Bower asked.

"She does not. She doesn't know anything about Teufel's earlier trip. A friend in the RCMP found the information for me."

Again Bower was silent for a few seconds.

"I think Teufel had the hots for Calloway. I know he'd met her first, and there was something about him on the climb. Call it a bad vibe. I don't know the guy that well. "But I guess I could believe he'd do that. Teufel did seem always to be watching Patty and Tif.

"You know I didn't say anything at the time, but that accident seemed off. The chance of a rock falling the way that rock did were a million to one."

As I hung up the phone, I felt as if someone were watching me. Out of the corner of my eye, I thought I saw a familiar figure standing in the far corner of the room. I turned, but my office was empty.

○

I had very mixed emotions as I entered the climbing gym as I was now convinced that Teufel had murdered Tif. My dream had been, after all, a dream. Speaking to Bower convinced me. Teufel had a motive—he was in love with Patty Ann Calloway. And now I knew he had the opportunity.

Somehow, though, I managed to greet him with a smile when I met him after dressing in the Locker room.

"Hey," he said. "You ready to learn top-roping?"

"All set," I said, indicating my harness with a downward motion of my hands.

"Let me check that out," he said. He checked my harness and said to tighten the leg loops. "You are going to be glad I sold you a padded one," he said.

He led me over to a wall in an area I had not been in before. Here the ceiling of the gym was the highest I'd seen. The colored climbing holds rising along the wall entered a narrowing tower that ended over fifty feet above me.

From a metal device on the top, two long ends of a climbing rope descended to the padded floor.

"Now your harness is on correctly and secured to your body. What's going to happen today is you're going to climb to the top of this tower with this safety rope attached.

"You will have one end of this rope," he said, holding out one end of a rope he held in his hand, "attached to your harness. As you can see," he pointed upward, "the rope goes up through that anchor at the top called a top anchor. I will be controlling the other end of the rope down here.

°

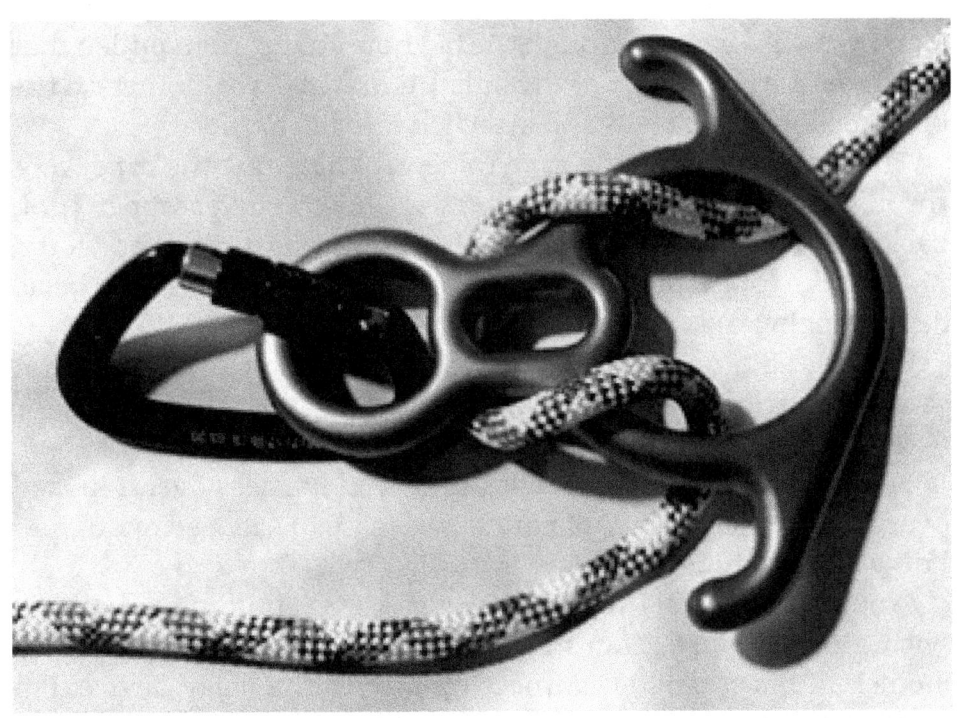

°

"What I'll be doing is called belaying. Now the gym has auto belayers, machines that can belay for you, but there would be no such thing on a real climb. Here I'll be controlling the rope. As you climb, I'll be giving you slack in the rope. But only enough that if you fall, you won't fall far. If you fall, I'll be holding this end of the rope to stop you from falling."

He spent the next several minutes instructing me on how to tie a figure-eight knot that would affix my end of the climbing rope to my harness. Then he added an extra knot at the end. "This is a backup knot," Martin said. "It prevents the figure eight from slipping. It's redundant. I love redundancy."

He then showed me how he set up the rappel device. The device, also called a rescue figure eight, was basically shaped like a number 8 with horns and an extra smaller loop in the center. It resembled, I thought, because of the horns, a flat bull. The horns were what made the rescue 8 different from a normal figure 8.

Martin pushed a loop through the big hole on top, then pulled that loop over the lower part of the bull. He snapped a carabiner on the bottom loop of the eight and attached it to his harness.

The device pinched the rope to control how fast the rope went through the device. He then showed me how to tie a stopper knot, basically just a big knot, near his end of the rope that would prevent the rope from escaping him by running through the belay device unchecked.

The whole time I felt as if he was studying me. And it did not seem like a friendly scrutiny.

Finally, Martin said, "Now we inspect each other's work."

Martin looked my figure-eight knot and harness over. I looked over his belay setup but, of course, wasn't experienced enough to know if everything was okay.

"You know, when I was a teenager, I was climbing in Austria with a boy my age, Han's Felter. He was my belayer. I spotted a crack in his carabiner connecting him to the belay device. I'm pretty sure it saved my life that day. Apparently, he liked a girl I was dating."

I looked into his eyes then. Had he mentioned that attempt by his climbing partner to cause an accident for a reason? I had no idea if that was a true story, but that didn't matter. I was pretty sure he was trying to find out if I suspected him of anything. So, I just smiled.

Just as I started scanning the wall, concentrating on some large jug grips that would start me on my way, Marin asked casually, "You know Patty Calloway?"

Luckily for me, I was ready for the question. I had expected him to ask about Patty. And I had wondered how he would broach it. Obviously, he'd tried to blindside me with the question.

"Yes," I said, turning, looking Martin in the eye. If I was not mistaken, I sensed enmity there. "I was looking for a house to put up a relative I might have to care for, and I needed to find out if she would be claiming part or all of the house she inherited from Tif."

"No," Martin said, "she gave the house to her boyfriend's brother. Thatch left her rather well-off with the insurance he'd purchased."

"That's what I learned," I said and looked at Martin. I knew there was a hidden question behind the smile he forced. "Anyway, I told her that I had acquired a painting by Tif, and she asked to see it."

I didn't try to tell him she had come to my house to see the painting. It would be better if he figured that out for himself. But my heart was hammering.

"So, yes, I do know her," I said. "But not very well. Are you good friends with her?"

"We are," he said. He almost made it sound like a question as if he suspected I might have had something to do with her avoiding him.

"Now, on this wall, you can only prepare for your climb based on what you can see from where you are. So study the wall and plan your moves for your start. Then, when you get as far as you've planned for, look ahead and do it again."

I examined the wall and planned the first part of my ascent. Then I looked at Martin.

"Ready?" he asked. I sensed relief in his voice.

"On belay?" I asked using the term he taught me—it was the question the climber asked the belayer to see if the belayer was ready.

"Belay on," Martin replied.

"Climbing," I said. Indicating I was going to start.

"Climb on," Martin replied. I began climbing.

Previously, I had not had my feet higher than about 8 feet on the 12-foot bouldering wall. As I ascended above 20 feet on this wall, I began to feel a little uneasy.

Below me, Martin was careful to allow just a few feet of slack as I climbed. The way he watched me made me uneasy.

I looked down at the rope attached to my harness and wondered if it would, in fact, hold me if I slipped.

Somewhere I had read that the best thing to do was to concentrate on the next hold and avoid thinking of a possible fall. I looked at the choices of holds above me, chose the largest, and grabbed hold.

"Hold on using no more strength than necessary," Martin called out from below. "Use your legs, not your arms. If your arms get too pumped on a climb, then you're done for."

I looked down, avoiding looking at Martin for the moment. Instead, I studied the wall, found the next spot for my right foot, and moved my foot to it.

Martin had instructed me that if I began to fall, I was to call out 'Falling.' That was a standard for all climbers. "Or, 'Oh, Shit'," Martin added as a joke. The way Martin had looked at me earlier, I wondered if he'd actually do what he needed to do to break my fall.

Still, I kept 'falling' on the tip of my tongue.

At 30 feet, I discovered they'd written the height on the wall. As I passed the '40 feet' sign, I began to feel definitely nervous. Even with padding below me, a fall from this height could fracture ribs, maybe even break my neck if I landed wrong. But only about a foot-length of rope hung down from my harness, meaning that should I fall, it should not be far.

As I passed the 'fifty feet' sign, I saw that further on, there were smaller climbing holds. As I reached a purple jug that eased some of my fear, smaller climbing holds, some only inches wide and barely protruding from the wall, radiated outward like planets drifting away from the sun. The jug seemed to be the last large hold.

The air at the top of the tower felt warmer. The scent of sweat and chalk dust seemed to fill the air along with a woman's expensive perfume. A slight wave of dizziness sent my heart racing. The padded floor called from far below.

Perched less than six feet from the top, I knew that after a few more moves, I'd be going down. I knew I could always start my descent now. I didn't have to climb this wall. But something about Martin made me refuse to quit no matter how scared I felt.

"Use your left foot to edge that small gray knob near the jug you're holding," Martin commanded from below.

I looked at the wall and saw a thin bit of a gray-colored hold sticking out. 'Edge' meant I was to use the inside of my foot. I lifted my foot, turning the inside edge toward the wall, and put the ball of my foot and big toe on the hold.

"Now lift your right foot and smear the little outcrop to your right," Martin instructed.

I held on tightly and lifted my right foot, putting my toes on the side of the outcrop and pushing down in such a way that if I were touching a sponge full of paint, it would slide and 'smear' a linoleum floor.

"Don't hold so tight with your hands," Martin ordered. "Hold with as little strength as possible."

I loosened my grip on the jug.

"Now push yourself up, and to the right and grab that hand-sized yellow pinch with your right hand," Martin instructed.

Now a pinch is a hold you need to pinch down on as you grab it. I moved my left hand and put pressure on the smooth side of a blue breast-shaped hold. This gave me a bit of support as I reached for the pinch with my right hand. Pushing down with my legs, I threw myself up and got my right hand on the yellow thingamabob, and gripped it as tight as I could. But as I did so, my right foot slipped from the edge it had just been pushing on. My left hand had no real hold on the sloper it was on, as that hand was merely keeping me from tipping to the left. I had watched the 2019 Oscar-winning movie, Free Solo. Soon after his ascent of El Capitan, the movie showed Alex Hammond doing one-finger chin-ups for exercise. My fingers were nowhere near that strong, and I watched in horror as my fingers slipped from the pinch hold.

It seemed to take me a long time to get the cry, "Falling," out.

There is a cartoon about a coyote, Wild-E-Coyote, who is always failing to catch a bird known as a roadrunner. Often his attempts to catch the roadrunner, named Beep Beep, resulted in a long fall. But before the fall, Wild-E seems to be suspended in the air, as if given a moment by gravity to realize his fate.

An instant before I was descending, accelerating, 32 feet per second per second, I experienced a Wild-E-Coyote moment as I seemed to be suspended in the air, hovering above over 50 feet of nothingness. Only my wildly accelerating heart seemed to be moving.

And then I was swinging, suspended on my harness, dangling before the wall just a few feet or so lower than I had been a moment before.

I looked down. Martin was lowering his feet from the edge of the climbing wall, the force of my fall having lifted him slightly off the floor. The belay device was on his left. The rope was wrapped under his butt. Martin held the brake side of the rope tight in his right hand.

With his left hand, he held the rope above the figure-eight loosely.

"Try to yell, 'Falling,' a little louder next time," he said. "We are not in a church, and if you are outside, you need to be heard."

I found myself, heart beating like an old-fashioned coffee percolator where the stove had been turned up to high, unable to think or move.

"Grab one of the holds, then place your feet so that you can come down," Martin called from below.

I heard him, but I could not get my body to respond.

Then, almost suddenly, there was a climber beside me on my right. After seeing those other climbers race up the wall the first day I'd come to the gym, I was not surprised that he had gotten up to me so fast. His orange helmet was tipped toward me as he took my right hand and guided it toward a hold right in front of me. When I had that hold in hand, he gestured to a place to put my right foot. When my right foot was balanced on the narrow ledge, my fear dissipated enough to let me out of its stranglehold, and I was able to begin to move down at a snail's pace concentrating on my hand and foot placement the entire way.

"Well," Martin said when I was again safely on the mats. "You've had your first fall. If you continue climbing, it won't be your last."

I looked up at the wall and then around me. There was no one anywhere near us. "Who was that climber who helped me?" I asked.

Martin Teufel looked at me as if I were crazy. "What climber? There's been nobody over here but us," he said.

I didn't know what to say, so I said nothing.

After a long silence, Martin looked me directly in the eye. "That's it for today. Do you want to keep going? With the lessons? I'll understand if you want to quit."

"Yes," I said though my mind was telling me to say no. 'Let's keep going."

"Well, then," he held out his hand.

I noticed that a young woman with blonde hair tied back in a ponytail, with a pretty face and blue eyes, had come up and was standing behind Martin.

I extended my hand, and Martin shook it, saying, "Congratulations, on your first fall," he said. "I have another lesson now, so if you'll excuse me, I'll see you tomorrow." He squeezed hard enough for me to know just how strong his hands actually were.

o

Knowing Martin would be busy with his student gave me the opportunity to talk to Patty Calloway again without having to worry about Martin going over to her house and seeing me there. It was late enough that even if she'd held band practice today, she'd most likely be home.

As I drove to Patty's house, I wondered about the climber who had helped me get a grip and get back on the wall. He had looked as solid as you or me. But then, how had he simply vanished, and why hadn't Martin noticed him? He had to have gone over the top of the wall, I decided. I just couldn't believe that it had been Tif's ghost that helped me. And Martin not seeing him meant that Martin hadn't been paying as much attention as he should.

A half-hour after I'd left Martin at the gym, I stood in front of Patty Calloway's door. For a moment, I stood there as if frozen. I had this sense of Déjà vu. Patty hadn't lived in this house before the climb. She'd lived in the house she shared with Tif. So, there was no reason that I, dreaming as Tif, would remember this house. But as I stood there, I was reminded of standing outside my wife Autumn's door when I picked her up for our first date. That memory of Autumn helped me understand that my dreams were making my feeling for the real Patty Calloway confused. I forced myself to ring the doorbell.

When Patty Ann Calloway opened her doo, she smiled. "Hi," she said and gave me a questioning look.

I held out the copy of the file that Hamil had made.

"Did you know that Martin Teufel went to Ungacongagru right after your plans for the climb had been finalized?" I asked.

For a moment, she looked confused. "I told you Martin is a friend," she said.

"Did you know John Bower thinks Martin might have set up Tif's accident?" I asked.

She just looked at me for a second, then said, "I don't want to hear this. Martin is my friend," and with that, she shut the door.

"I dreamt that Martin murdered Tif!" I shouted at the top of my lungs.

No sound came from behind the door.

I stood there for a moment fighting the urge to knock, kick the door open and shake some sense into her. But I didn't see myself doing that. And I knew that wouldn't help, as she'd never believe me. Instead, I put the folder down on the doormat, hoping she'd see it and look at it, and then walked back to my car.

°

I felt I needed to find out more from the members of the climb. I hadn't reached Peter Lambas or Jessie Bock, and I thought I'd better talk to all the members of that climbing group.

Again I dialed Lambas first. There was no answer after five rings, and the mailbox was still full. Go figure--a physicist not knowing how to clear his phone's voicemail.

Jesse Bock answered on the fourth ring. He had a deep, firm voice that belied the fact he was only 22 at the time of the climb and the youngster of the group.

I went through my psychologist routine with more sincerity than I had with Bower. Bock seemed to be buying it and said, "I'll be glad to help Patty anyway I can."

"Was there anything funny about the way Tif died?" I asked. "There seems to be something bothering her about it that she can't quite put a handle on."

"Well, it was a terrible tragedy," Bock replied. "And I can understand her being upset. After all, she got engaged the night before." He paused as if thinking.

"And she and all the rest of us were very lucky," Bock added.

"How were you lucky?" I asked.

"We were all anchored at a rest stop when Tif fell. If he had fallen while we were climbing, we might all have been pulled off the mountain."

We chatted for about ten minutes. What he told me about the climb pretty much matched what Land Donahue had said. When I felt I had created a rapport with Bock, it was time to go ahead and ask Bock the million-dollar question.

"Some of the other members of the climb have told me that the accident might not have been an accident at all," I said.

"What do you mean not an accident?" Bock asked, sounding confused.

"Well," I said. "Some of the people I talked to were surprised to learn that Martin Teufel went to Ungacongagru the August before the climb, right after the climb was finalized."

There was a silence on the line. "Nah," Bock said. "Who the hell told you that?"

"It's a matter of public record. He picked up climbing equipment in Calgary and flew to the Stony Nakoda Resort," I said evenly. It was hard to keep the excitement out of my voice. I was supposed to be a psychologist, not a detective.

"That doesn't mean he went to Ungacongagru ahead of us," Bock was protesting now. "I know Martin. Sure he had a thing for Patty Calloway and was upset she got engaged to Tif. But he met her first, and I didn't think Tif had any business going after her."

"Doubts about Tif's death being an accident could be what is upsetting Ms. Calloway," I said. "Do you think Mr. Teufel would have the skill to set up an accident on the mountain? Would he be capable of harming Tif?"

There was a long silence on the other end of the line. Then, when Bock finally spoke, he was blatantly angry. "Who the hell did you say you were again?"

"I am a psychologist treating Ms. Calloway for symptoms somewhat like Post Traumatic Stress Disorder that have manifested themselves since Mr. Febbron died."

"Give me your name and contact info," Bock demanded.

"Certainly," I said. The reason I had picked the name of my old teacher, Dr. Bauilding, was that I had anticipated this. Luckily, Bauilding was a retired psychologist in Missoula whose web page information was still available but who was no longer residing in Missoula. He now resided in Spanish Wells in the Bahamas without internet or a cell phone. The Doc had taught at the university and had been one of my favorite teachers. I gave Bock his name and the web link.

"Listen," I said. "I've obviously upset you. Why don't I let you look at my credentials if you feel you need to do that. You can contact me at this number if you want to."

"I'll do that," Bock said. "Good day."

He hung up before I could thank him or say goodbye. I knew he would not get far with any inquiry about Doc. What I did not expect was what he did do.

DAY 10: TUESDAY

°

I woke in the morning from a dream in which I was at Tif's funeral. It was a blustery day, and the trees in the small cemetery waved in the breezes. Martin Teufel and the five other male members of the climb on Ungacongagru were the pallbearers. The air smelled of pine and woodsmoke.

The bearers looked somber as they carried the coffin and laid it down on the straps crossing the top of a brass frame around the grave. A sparkle of sunlight winked on the casket as the leaves above stirred.

Patty Calloway sat with an older woman. Tears streamed down from both women's eyes. I imagined the woman to be Tif's mother. Tif's brother, Timothy, stood on Patty's other side. I watched as Martin Teufel eased himself between Timothy and Patty Ann so as to be standing next to her. I felt an anger surge through me at the sight. Then I woke.

The mists in the painting swirled almost angrily as I opened my eyes. And then I saw Tif standing by the painting, again. Dressed for a climb, he wore a climbing harness. Cams, carabiners, and a rescue 8 hung from his sides. He held a helmet in his hands. My heart was hammering in my chest. He did not say as much as mouth the words. 'Help her!'

I turned to get out of bed, to go and confirm he was real, but though I had only turned away for an instant, Tif was gone.

o

That afternoon Martin took me to a part of the climbing gym I hadn't seen before.

"First, let me show you how to coil a rope," he said. He showed me quickly how to loop a long climbing rope so that two easy-to-straighten coils hung from over both shoulders.

Then, after we'd both chalked up, he urged me to climb with him up the slanted rather than vertical wall, to a platform about six feet wide and four deep, 18 feet above the mats.

"Today," Martin said, "I'm going to teach you how to rappel. It's called abseiling in Europe. Basically, it's one way to get down.

He then pointed to the floor where three types of anchors were secured to the faux stone platform: a bolt with a metal loop, a piton hammered into a crack, and a cam secured to a wider crack. Each had a carabiner attached.

o

Martin pointed to the bolt and piton, "These two are for show and actually welded to the metal frame of the platform. The cam is real enough," he added, squeezing the sides of the device. Three half circles on individual spindles, which were wedged into the crack, moved from horizontal to vertical, allowing him to remove the device from the crack. "Pitons were damaging many climbing sites, so the tendency now is to use removable anchors," he added, as he squeezed the cam, put it back in the crack, then let go, so it expanded.

I examined the three ropes that connected to one of the three anchors and then joined together, individually, on a ring. We would secure the rope that we would be using for our lesson in rappelling to that ring.

"If you want to live, make sure you have at least three anchors. Redundancy means safety."

I guessed what he was going to say next and said it at the same time he did, "I love redundancy."

Martin looked at me and smiled. "There is this knot called a Munter Knot you can use for rappelling, but it twists the rope up. You never know when you might accidentally drop your rappelling device. In a future lesson, I'm going to teach you how to rappel with just that knot and its big brother, the super Munter, but we'll save that for another day.

Martin picked up a shorter coil of blue rope, long enough to reach the floor and back again, and threaded it through the ring. When he was done, the mid-point was at the ring, and both ends were on the floor.

"When climbing, you'd use a dynamic rope. That is, you'd want a rope that can stretch, so if you fall, it reduces the pressure on you and the rope when you hit the end.

"But here we can use a static rope—a rope that doesn't stretch— because you will, we hope, be keeping constant pressure on it.

°

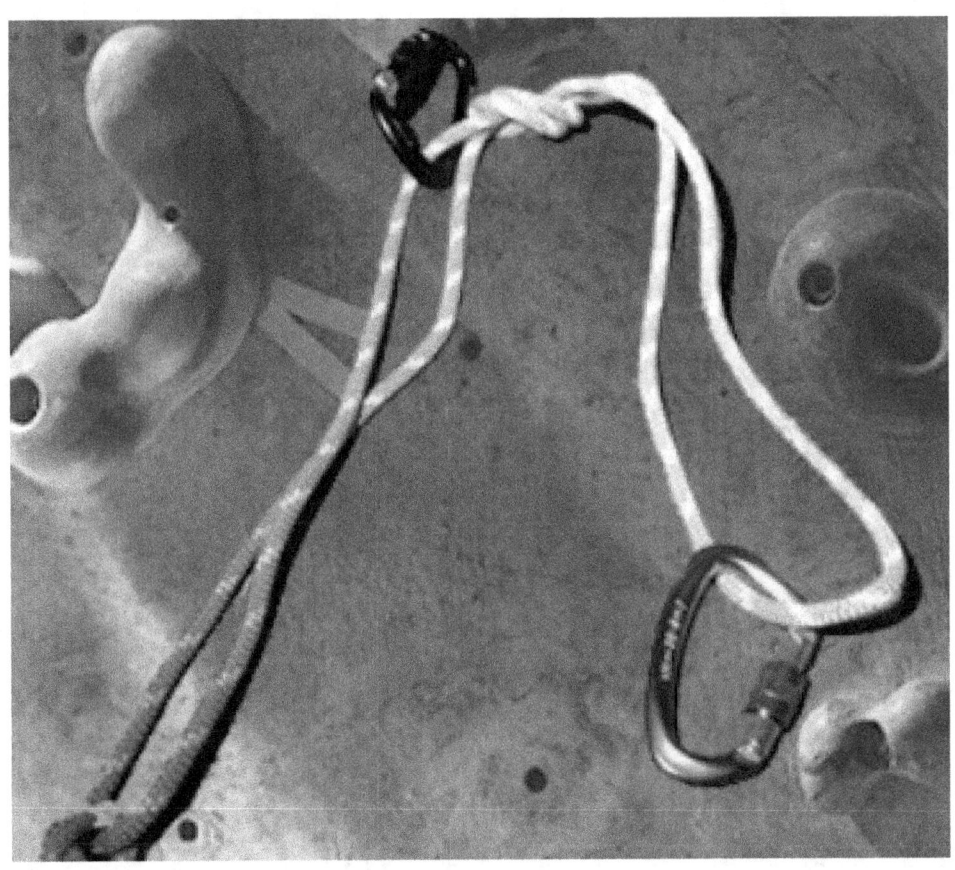

°

"Today, I'm going to show you first how to use an extension. You'll use a loop of rope." He held out a loop of rope with the ends tied together to make a 40-inch loop.

"I'll be using this," he said, holding out a 40-inch loop made from a thin version of the kind of straps that hold loads down on flatbed trucks. "You will be doing with the rope what I'm doing with this thing that looks like it was made from a dog's leash."

I laughed, realizing it did, in fact, looked like the main strap of a dog's leash sewn into a circle.

"Now tie a knot in your extension about two-thirds of the way up," he said and did the same with his dog-leash-like extension.

He demonstrated on himself. Instead of looping the extension through the loop in the front of his harness, his belay loop, he ran one end through the loop his belay loop was attached to by his legs, and then the loop his belay loop was attached to, at his waist. He then ran the loop of the extension through itself. Now he had an open loop attached to his harness. He then tied a knot in the center.

"Now you attach a carabiner to the far end," he said, doing so. "Then attach that carabiner to your anchor until you are ready to descend." He hooked the carabiner at the end of the loop to the anchor ring and gestured for me to do the same.

°

o

"Hooking to the anchor is protection to keep you from falling as you set up," Martin explained. "Then another carabiner goes on the lower side of the knot you tied in the middle, and this is the one we'll hook to what is called a 'tubular belay device.' The device resembled a bell-shaped lock with two chambers and holes at the top of each chamber for a rope to poke through. Martin pressed both lines of our rope into the chambers, then slipped a carabiner around the rope.

o

o

"Like the figure 8, this simple little device is great for rappelling as well as belaying. With it, you can insert two sides of the same rope. That way, when you reach the ground, you can just pull your rope down from the anchor. Otherwise, you have to go back up to untie it.

"For today, just hold the rope below the rappel device with your stronger hand--in your case, your right.

"Now, are you ready?" he asked.

At my nod, he unhooked the carabiner attached to the anchor. "Rappel!"

o

I backed up to the edge of the platform with the 18-foot drop behind me. My heart was racing. At Martin's urging, I took a step back. The rope held me. My left hand held the rope going to the anchors above me like I'd never gripped anything before. My stronger right hand kept pressure on the rope below the knot to control the speed of my descent.

"Don't hold on so tight," Martin ordered. "Only hold on with just enough strength. You might someday have a long way to go, and you don't want your hands cramping."

I took another step, letting out just a bit more rope. I repeated that. By the time I was halfway down, standing almost perpendicular to the wall, I was calming down. I got down, and it felt great to be standing on level ground.

"Okay," Martin called from above, "Let's do it again."

Pretty soon, I was walking myself down the 3-fathom wall with confidence. I made six trips with the rappelling device, and it was fun.

At the end of my last rappel, Martin, who had joined me on the gym floor, said, "Now this is why it's nice to have two ends of the same rope hanging down." With that, he pulled on one of the rope ends. The other end went up, slipped through the anchor ring, and came back down.

We'd finished my lesson, and his other student was standing nearby, anxious to begin hers.

"Listen," Martin said, "I don't have any lessons but yours tomorrow. My usual student has a doctor's appointment, so what say we go out and get a lesson on rappelling in the real world?"

"I guess," I said.

"Good," Martin said.

I would meet him at 10 in the morning, but instead of the climbing gym, we'd meet at the entrance to Rattler Gulch off the frontage road not far from Drummond.

o

Just after 11 that evening, I was reading in my den when someone began a persistent knocking on my front door. Normally, I would just go and answer the door, but whoever was pounding on it with some energy. I keep a pistol by my bed, a .357 magnum revolver. I do live remotely, and as my home makes it obvious that I am wealthy, I feel the protection is reasonable.

As I fetched my revolver, the doorbell rang.

Then it began ringing over and over.

I had no experience with crazy people at my door. A disgruntled author who did not get the response they wanted to their ad did not seem likely. They usually came to the office.

I approached my door with caution. And in deference to whomever it might be (should it be, for example, a policeman), I hid the gun behind my back as I swung the front door open and stepped back, ready to bring the gun forward if need be.

A serious-looking Patty Ann Calloway stood in the doorway staring at me. "Have you been calling people in my climbing party, telling them that you're my therapist who's treating me for post-traumatic stress disorder?" she asked. She didn't seem overly angry about it.

The first moment's surprise must have allowed a flash of guilt to cross my face before I could muster a poker face.

Besides, the feelings I'd built up about the woman before me, even if they were due to dreams, could not fail to influence me in how I responded to her.

I admit it; I was infatuated.

Anyway, I was pretty sure she now knew I was the culprit and pushed her way past me into my foyer.

A thousand replies flashed through my mind. But loathe to confess, I asked. "Did you read the file I left by your door?"

She ignored my question.

"Are you even a therapist?" she demanded.

"No..." I started. Then I realized this line of questioning and any reply I might give to it was not going to help me get this woman to see Matin Teufel as the murderer he was.

"I dreamt how Martin murdered Tif," I said. "He unhooked his carabiner from the rope team and crawled along a ledge to a long flat stone he had set in place. He set the accident up when he visited Ungacongagru secretly months before. The pitch Tif was climbing was slanted at an angle. He was the last climber. When he came around a small overhang, Martin pushed the stone off the ledge, and there was no way Tif could get out of the way."

"In this dream, did you know why Martin did that?" she asked.

"Because he wanted you," I answered.

For a long time, she just stood there. Then, to my total surprise, Patty began to cry. I moved to her, touched her arm. She did not push me away.

"You believe me?" I asked.

The woman before me shook her head as her right hand went to wipe away her tears.

I gave her a questioning look.

"I don't want to. But I did read the file you left by my door, and then last night I had a dream about the accident," she said. "But in my dream, it was you instead of Thatch I found hanging, injured at the end of the rope."

As we stepped into my living room, Patty said, "Martin was just at my house. I came here as soon as he left."

According to Patty, Martin was Jessie Bock's climbing mentor. It was Martin who invited the mostly inexperienced Bock on the climb. The Martin who came to her door had been so furious, Patty had been scared. And she suddenly realized he was not the calm, compassionate man she had thought him to be.

She had read Hamil's report and knew there was something seriously wrong with the fact that he had not mentioned visiting Ungacongagru before the actual climb. But she had been afraid to confront a raging Martin about that. Instead, she played along and told Martin that she had no idea who had been pretending to be her therapist. She kept to her story even when Martin persisted, angrily, that she had to know. When she finally got him to leave after 10:30, she came to see me.

"You saw me as Tif in your dream?" I asked.

She nodded.

"Did you dream about the wake and the funeral?" I asked. "Martin kept insinuating himself next to you."

"No. But I didn't need to dream it," she said. "I was there. I thought at the time he was just being supportive. He took care of almost everything to do with the funeral."

"He's obsessed with you," I said.

"I think you're right," she said sadly. She thought for a few moments. "But how could we prove he actually did anything?"

"I have a lesson with him tomorrow. Rappelling on a boulder face in Rattler Gulch. Maybe I can get him to say something incriminating."

"Like what?" Patty asked.

"I can ask if he checks out climbs in advance," I said. "And move the conversation to Ungacongagru. If I can get him to admit to me that he went to Ungacongagru ahead of time, you can confront him about not telling anyone he had done that. Together, maybe we can push him enough that he slips up."

Patty did not look too happy. "Until tonight, I wouldn't have believed he could have done it. But after the report and seeing how he behaved tonight, I believe you now. I suppose it's worth a try."

"Could you follow me tomorrow?" I asked. "Or better yet, get there ahead of me? I can call you and leave my phone on. We can both record the conversation. Maybe we'll get really lucky and get enough to go to the authorities."

"So you were pretending to be my therapist?" Patty asked.

I looked at her for a long moment. "I have been dreaming about you since I got the painting. I've been Tif in my dreams, but I've also been me. As you know, I lost my wife some years ago. I miss her terribly. But then I started dreaming I was this man who you were in love with. I have feelings for you that I know are totally unrealistic because they are based on dreams.

I became scared for you because I believed Martin killed Tif to get you. I had to find out if my dream about Martin was what really happened. I had my computer tech guy get the information I left by your door. I figured if Martin did kill Tif, he had to set it up in advance. I found out about the trip he made. So, he had the opportunity. But that still wasn't enough.

I needed a way to get the members of your climbing team to talk to me. I was worried they'd refuse, so I made up the story about being your therapist."

She was looking at me, and her expression was unreadable.

"Can you forgive me?" I asked.

Patty looked down at the floor and said nothing for a long time. Then she said, "It isn't whether I can forgive you as much as whether I can trust you. I need to think about that."

DAY 11: WEDNESDAY

°

Patty didn't leave until 6 a.m., and so I never went to bed, and therefore there were no dreams that night. I went to the office to have something to do rather than just wait around for my climb with Martin.

I didn't accomplish a thing at the office, and I was a nervous wreck by the time I left and got into my car.

Turning off I-90 at the Bear Mouth exit, I made my way to the frontage road and drove toward Drummond.

At the turnoff to Rattler Gulch, I turned left and drove up by the turnoff to a ranch, so I was in sight of the frontage road and could see if Martin came along.

I took out my iPhone and called Patty's number. She answered just after the first ring.

"Hi," she said breathlessly.

"Hi. I'm parked on Rattler by the ranch road waiting for Martin. Are you here?" I asked.

"Yes. I'm driving up Rattler as we speak. I'm pretty sure he'll be taking you to Sheep Gulch. I'll hide my car further up, park, and walk back and find a good hiding spot in the climbing area before you two arrive."

"Be safe," I said, wanting to say more.

"I'll try," she replied. I heard her car door open and realized I had to turn the sound off on my phone. My hands actually shook.

Then I almost turned the phone off before realizing I needed to keep it on.

Less than 5 minutes later, Martin Teufel pulled up.

I got out of the car. Martin rolled down his driver's-side window.

"Not much further to go," he said. "Just follow me."

There was something about the way he looked at me that made me nervous. But I pretended to ignore it and walked back to my car.

Martin drove fast. We followed a narrow, two-way, dirt road that looked like it received quite a bit of traffic. We passed grassy hillsides covered in small trees, dilapidated buildings, and, at one point, a group of about twenty mule deer. Finally, the road meandered up a steeper-sided canyon road.

I sped up as Martin was already out of sight ahead of me.

Soon after I caught up, Martin pulled into a small turnoff under some trees. We'd reached Sheep Gulch. I pulled in next to him. There was no one else around.

"We seem to have the place to ourselves," Martin said, exiting his vehicle.

"No waiting," I said.

"Come on, let's get this show on the road. You have all your gear?"

"Yeah," I said.

"Let's get our gear on, and then we have a little walk ahead of us.," Martin said.

When we were both geared up, Martin carried the 60-meter

rope we'd be using and a bag. The rope looked like the same one he had shown me how to coil in the gym. He led the way. His helmet was the same color as the one he sold me, a bright orange. I followed it like a bouncing ball. At first, it was an easy walk up Rattler Gulch Road, rounding a few turns where it was apparent there were no closer parking spots. We then began walking up a steep, winding path through the trees along the side of an almost vertical monolith. I was winded when we topped out. The climb didn't seem to phase Martin at all.

It was as if a slice had been cut out of the top of the gigantic rock, creating a two-foot-wide ledge, with a low wall a few feet high on one side and a 30-meter drop on the other. Into the wall, three bolts had been set for rappellers to use as an anchor.

o

"What can you tell me about this anchor?" Martin asked.

"It has three bolts driven into the rock," I said.

Martin nodded, "Go on."

I touched the set-up. "Three straps are attached by locked carabiners, one to each bolt," I continued, "and the other ends of the straps are connected to three locked carabiners."

"Those are nylon straps and stainless steel carabiners," Martin said. "You'll notice there is no corruption of the metal. They are checked and replaced each spring. What these are primarily for is rappelling. Do you think this anchor is secure?"

"It sure looks like it," I said.

"Pull on each one," Martin ordered.

I lifted the carabiner strapped to the bolt on the left and pulled with all my strength. The strap held, and the bolt didn't move. I did the same for the other two. It seemed like it would take a great deal of force to break them or pull them loose.

"So, we have the first thing we need for safe rappelling, redundant, secure anchors," Martin said. "And you know I love redundancy."

I smiled.

"Now I have a gift for you. One I like to give to all my students," he said.

o

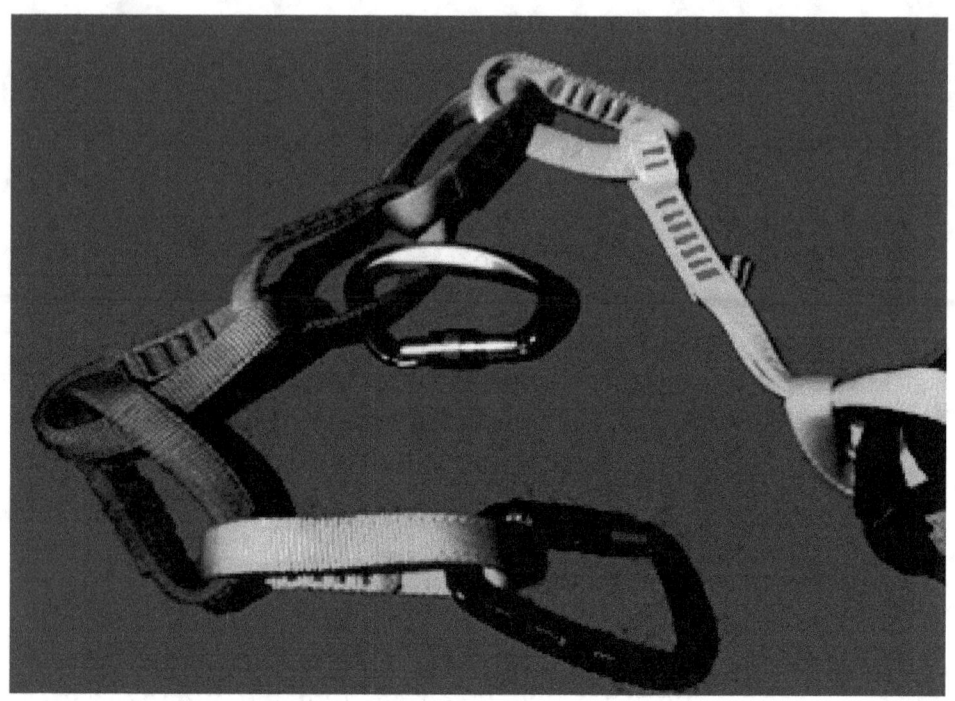

°

From the bag he had been carrying, he pulled a chain of colorful nylon loops. It seemed to be made of the same material as Martin's extender. Most of the loops were short and the same size but for the green one at one end, which was a little longer. The whole thing was over 3 feet long.

"This is an extension made from the same material as the one I used in the gym for rappelling. "It's called a SubZero Chain Extend; it is my favorite brand of what are commonly known as daisy extensions--because they look like a daisy chain," Martin said. "What's great about it is you don't need to tie knots into it. Knots actually weaken extension loops. This one doesn't need knots.

"Each link is sewn together and can support 25kN. That's twenty-five kilonewtons or 5,620 pounds (2.55 tons) of force. This thing is made to withstand the coldest temperatures on earth. It won't crack, even at -140 °F."

He watched me loop the green end to my harness and then hook a carabiner to the furthest link of the chain extension and secure the carabiner to all three of the anchor's carabiners.

"This daisy extension is my favorite, and I wanted you to have one," Martin said.

He then threaded half the 60-meter rope through the three anchor's carabiners. "Now I've marked the center of this rope, so I know the ends are even. But you should never take anyone's word for something like this. Always check yourself. You are secured to the anchors with the extender, so you are safe to lean out and check that both ends of the rope are on the ground below," Martin said.

Feeling secure with the extension hooked to the anchor, I peered over the edge. Both ropes ends were on the ground far below. I didn't even need to use the support of the anchor but having the extension attached to it, and my harness made me feel safe.

I took the tubular belay device I bought to use for my first rappel out of my bag.

"You got your own," Martin said. "Great, set it up."

I fit the two sides of the rope into the device. I hooked a carabiner between the loops and the device and then attached the carabiner to the middle loop on my daisy chain. After a thorough check, Martin nodded. "Looks good."

I detached the carabiner at the end of my daisy chain from the anchor. I then hooked that to a loop on my belt. I was only attached to the anchor by the ropes attached to my rappelling device.

"All set?" Martin asked.

I had been hesitating to ask the questions I needed to ask. I'd thought that I'd get to ask as we hiked to the top of the monolith, but Martin had taken the lead, and it had been hard for me to keep up with him, let alone talk. Once I had rappelled down, I was sure that Martin would be leaving. He told me that the lesson would just be one rappel down the cliff face.

"I was curious," I said. "When you do a climb, do you always go out and check the mountain ahead of time?"

"Almost always," Martin said, easily.

It was then I felt my heart stop. For an instant, beside Martin, stood the man I had seen in my bedroom. The man I knew to be Thatcher Ian Febbron. He was glaring at Martin.

"I do have another place to be. Start backing up. Let's make sure the device is working."

I looked at Martin. When I looked back, Tiff was gone. Holding the double rope, I took a short step back to the edge of the cliff.

"If you did that for Ungacongagru, didn't you notice the rock that hit Tif?" I asked.

"Okay," Martin said, ignoring my question for the moment, "Now on this rock, you need to ease over the lip."

I stepped slowly backward toward the lip, holding the double rope with my left hand above the rappel tube and my right below it.

"Don't hold on so tight," Martin instructed. "Let the harness hold you."

I began the tricky step over the lip, still gripping the rope as tightly as I could. Martin hadn't offered any advice at all on how to maneuver over the lip. After I'd descended a few feet and was hanging over the rocks almost 30 meters below, Martin said, "Of course I noticed the rock that killed Tif.

"It took me a long time to move that heavy rock into position, so I could make it fall when I needed to. Unlike you, Tif was an expert climber. I needed to plan his accident carefully.

"And as for you, this is your last climb."

I had no idea what Martin could have done to the equipment I was using, but I suddenly knew he had sabotaged it, and I was going to fall. What filled my mind was that he had cut or weakened the rope. I hadn't examined the rope. But it made no sense he would tamper with it. Wouldn't someone notice a cut or doctored rope?

"Jessie Bock called me after you talked to him," Martin continued, his voice now filled with contempt. "He didn't know who you were, pretending to be Patty's therapist as you did. But he warned me. I went to Patty and confronted her. She told me she didn't know who was doing it. But then I waited and followed her. She went directly to your house.

"It is a real problem for me that she likes you."

He stepped closer and looked down at me. He looked at my hands and smiled. "The only thing holding you up now are your hands, really. It is astonishing what a little liquid nitrogen can do to the threads holding the links of your SubZero daisy chain extender together. It may have been made for subzero temperatures but not for -320 F°. I thought it might fall apart, and you might fall off when you looked over the edge to check on the ropes, but you didn't lean out and put pressure on it as I had hoped.

"Someone will notice it was tampered with," I said feebly.

Martin laughed. "It's technically illegal in this country as it's made in North Korea. No one will question it falling apart.

"You're only holding on with your hands now, and they're not going to be holding on forever.

"Don't worry about Patty. I'll be gone on a trip for a time, but then I'll be back to console her. I'm sure she'll learn of your fall while I'm gone. She doesn't believe I had anything to do with Tif's death, and she never will once you are out of the way."

I heard the sound of his footsteps over the rocks. He was walking away. Fear gripped me. I tightened my grip on the ropes. I didn't dare look down. I don't know how long I hung there, but I heard Martin as he reached the road and walked toward his car. I knew then he hadn't told anyone about this lesson. He probably assumed I had no reason to tell anyone about it. In which case, no one would know he was even here. Everyone would think I had come here to try rappelling on my own.

Patty was my only hope now. She was here somewhere. I just hope she'd know how to rescue me. Waiting for her, I felt paralyzed and unable to move or even think, and then something seemed to take over me.

Almost involuntarily and incredibly, I found myself lifting my right leg over the rope and using it as a brake. I descended a few feet. Then, instead of going down, I found myself walking sideways along the cliff face. I saw handholds on the rock face and a tiny ledge I could get my right toe on to the right of me. I moved in that direction with my heart racing. As my right foot reached for the ledge, the first link of my chain extender separated. It was the link next to the one attached to the belay loop on my climbing harness. My body dropped an inch or so. But I was able to grab the hold I saw with my right hand and catch the ledge with my toe.

As I balanced myself on the ledge, a link at the other end of the daisy extender fell apart. Martin had doctored the second link at each end.

"Kevin!" I heard a voice cry out below me.

"Kevin, are you alright?" Patty called up.

"So far, so good," I said. Remembering the story of the optimist who fell from a 50-story building, saying as he passed each floor, 'So far so good.'

"I can see you've got your right foot on a ledge. Without losing the rope, can you move further to your right?" Patty asked.

I looked at my left hand. It still held the rope in a stranglehold.

"I don't know," I said.

"You have to try," she called.

I turned to my right, and Thatcher Ian Febbron was on the wall next to me. He pointed to a handhold a little further to the right and above the ledge, Patty had mentioned. Then he pointed at my right foot. I understood.

I put my weight on the handhold I gripped in my right hand and then slid my right foot a bit further over along the ledge. Now there was room for my left foot, and I moved it over to the ledge. With both feet on the ledge, I was able to reach for the handhold Tif's ghost was pointing to.

With Tif pointing out the holds, I managed to get myself over to a wider part of the ledge that I could actually stand on without holding on to the cliff face.

"Okay," Patty shouted from below. "I heard everything Martin said on my phone. He tried to kill you, but I think you can climb down from there."

"Climb?" I cried. "I've never climbed on a real boulder." I thought a moment. "Can't I hook the rappelling device to the belay loop on my harness and keep rappelling?"

"Did Martin give you that device?" Patty asked.

"No," I said. "I brought my own."

"What are you using that Martin brought?" Patty called up.

"Just the daisy chain," I said. Then remembered, "And the rope."

Patty shook her head. "We can't trust that he didn't sabotage the rope," she said. "Martin has a thing about redundancy. He probably had a backup plan in case the daisy chain-breaking didn't kill you. And you are using his rope. Can you wait a minute?" Patty asked. "I need to go to my car and get my harness. I can help you climb down."

"I have nothing better to do, I guess," I said.

"Glad you still have a sense of humor," Patty replied with a laugh. "I'll hurry back."

With that, she was gone, and I dared look down below me. My near fall had taken my confidence away. I looked around me. There was no sign of Tif's ghost. Tif, for now, was gone, as was Patty. I stood there, in no immediate danger of falling but terrified of falling anyway. Getting down seemed impossible. A breeze began to pick up and stir the branches on the pines on the other side of Rattler Gluch.

The seconds and minutes until Patty came back seemed like an eternity. Then finally, I heard her feet running back toward me.

"Can you get your rappel device free from the rope?" Patty asked breathlessly.

The rappel device was resting against my chest. The loose ends of the chain extension dangling from the carabiner like small flags and waving about in the breeze. I detached the carabiner from the loops of the rope and freed the rappel device.

"Okay," Patty said. "Attach the carabiner through the big loop on the device and then around both strands of the rope. When it's secure, send the rappel device down to me."

I did as I was told and sent the device down. Patty broke its fall by pulling the ends of the rope apart as it got to the bottom.

"Do you know how to tie a figure-eight knot to your harness?"

Patty asked.

"Yes," I said.

"Good," Patty said. "I'm going to start pulling on one end of the rope; let the rope run through your fingers but don't let go of either end. The side of the rope I am pulling on will come up toward you. Don't let it get past you! When the end gets to you, take it and tie a figure-eight knot to your harness."

"I can do that," I said.

Patty took her time pulling on the end of the rope. But still, as the rising end of the rope came close, my fingers fumbled. I watched the rope slip out of my hands. For a second, I froze, but then, I threw my left hand out and caught it. My heartbeat wildly.

I carefully tied the loose end of the rope in a figure eight to my harness. I pulled it tight, then called out with relief, "What now?"

"We can use the rope for belaying you and hope it holds if we need it," Patty called back. "But mostly, you're going to have to climb down. I'll belay you as best I can."

Then Tif was back again. He pointed to a lower ledge just a little way down. Then he guided my hands to two new handholds.

I don't remember most of the climb down. I vaguely remember finding cracks and ledges to get my finger and toes on. The things I'd learned in the climbing gym helped me. Somewhere near the bottom, Tif's ghost disappeared. I guess Tif thought I could do the last part well enough on my own.

When I was safely on the ground, I grabbed Patty and hugged her. She hugged me back. It took her a while to get me to finally let her go.

When I looked at her, she gave me a sad look. "I was kind of hoping Martin hadn't done it."

○

An hour later, Detective John Robertson waved us into chairs as he sat across from us in the conference room at police headquarters. The place must have also served as a lunchroom. A soda machine hummed between a snack machine and a fridge. A coffee machine held two almost full pots of coffee. The air smelled of coffee and something like a baloney sandwich.

"Can I get you a coffee?" The giant of a man asked. He must have been 6'6" and had dark wavy hair that seemed a bit mussed. His penetrating brown eyes first looked at me and then Patty. He had a bluish mole in the center of his right cheek that gave him a lopsided look.

"No," I said and looked at Patty.

"No, thank you," Patty said.

"You're here to report a murder?" Robertson asked.

"It didn't happen here," Patty said, taking out her phone and putting it down on the table in front of the detective. "But this man, Martin Teufel, a Missoula resident, murdered my fiancé. He admits it in this recording and then today, while this was being recorded, tried to kill Mr. Frost here."

"What's your relationship," Robertson asked, looking from one of us to the other. "If you don't mind me asking." It was clear from his tone he didn't care if we minded at all. He was just being superficially polite.

"We're acquaintances," I replied. "We met because of a painting by the victim, Thatcher Ian Febbron."

"Febbron," Robertson said. "I had heard he died sometime after a climbing accident."

"He was murdered," I said. "This recording proves it."

Patty had set up the recording to begin at the incriminating part. We had left my phone, and my copy at my office locked in the office safe.

John Robertson listened to our tape. I could tell by the way his forehead creased and his eyebrows rose that the conversation bothered him. When the recording had played, he switched the phone off.

"We have a problem," he said. "Are you aware that it is illegal in Montana to record a conversation without the other party knowing?" You can be arrested for doing it.

Both Patty and I looked at the man, stunned by his apparent indifference to a murder.

"Don't get me wrong," Robertson said. "I'd arrest the guy in an instant, but I can't. Not without evidence, we can use in court." He thought for a moment, then asked, "Where did this crime occur?"

"The murder took place in Canada," I said.

"On Ungacongagru," Patty said.

"In Canada?" Robertson asked.

Patty and I nodded.

"I don't know about the law in Canada. And since this is on a cell phone, maybe that's a good thing. Is there any indication in the recording about where the call was taped?"

He looked at both of us. We shook our heads, no.

He sighed. "I can send the recording to the Royal Canadian Mounted Police, and they might be able to arrest him based on their laws. But I'm not sure.

"But, sending the recording there without indicating that the conversation was taped in the Drummond area might negate your claim that the man tried to murder you today. Do you understand that?"

"I guess so," I said.

"As to your claim of attempted murder, it would be your word against his without the recording," Robertson said.

"There's the daisy chain he gave me that he rigged to fall apart," I said.

"Again, without the recording, you have no proof he did that," Robertson said.

Patty and I had come to the police station together in my car after she made a stop at her house to change. I took her home. We were both so disappointed, we barely spoke on the ride.

As I pulled up in front of her house, I said, "When I was on the cliff with Martin, I saw Tif."

Patty just looked at me.

"He helped me, showed me how to get to that little ledge where you found me," I added.

She didn't say anything for a long time. "Maybe the Canadians will get Martin," Patty finally said.

I looked into her eyes. "We can hope so," I said.

I walked her to her door.

We stood on her doorstep as if reluctant to part.

"You saved my life," I said. "That makes me your slave forever."

Patty smiled weakly. "I think it makes me responsible for you forever."

We stood there for a few more awkward moments. "I'd better go," I said.

"Call me," Patty said as I turned to go.

I looked back at her.

"If you hear anything," she said. I nodded and left.

○

I went straight home and got my .357. I had a concealed carry permit, so it wasn't illegal to hide the holster. I have to admit now I wasn't thinking clearly. But I was going to confront Martin Teufel.

There was no one at his home. I found the address easily enough, but there was no reply to my knock or the bell ringing.

I drove to the climbing gym. It was open late. I wasn't thinking so much about what might happen as what I might say. I wanted to see the expression on his face when I walked up to him.

I searched the gym, but I didn't see any sign of Martin. I did see Jeanette Brown. She was talking to two young teenagers whom she was obviously instructing. She excused herself and walked over to me.

"Can I help you with something, Mr. Frost?" she asked with a smile.

"I'm looking for Martin," I said. "Have you seen him?"

"He's gone to Mexico on a climb," Jeanette said. "Didn't he tell you that yesterday? He said he'd have to postpone the rest of your lessons until he got back."

○

I was so angry I thought about stopping at a bar on the way home but decided not to. I didn't need to be drunk.

DAY 12: THURSDAY

○

I tried reading in bed, but it took me a long time to get to sleep.

My ordeal the day before had been terrifying. But I'm not sure the dream I had that night wasn't as disturbing.

I was near the end of a narrow flat summit that reminded me of a chisel's top in gray stone. I was watching a climber ascend the rock face below me. He would top the chisel about a dozen feet further along from where I was standing. I watched him climb without any rope or other aid. He was free soloing.

And as I watched, I realized that I was filled with anger. The sun was behind me, but I cast no shadow on the short ridge ahead of me. My anger seemed to build until it seethed within me.

The man was less than ten feet below the summit when I saw that the climber was Martin Teufel. And I knew that this was something my dream persona already knew. Because in the dream,

I moved to intercept Martin as he pulled himself up to the top. He turned away from me as the peak's tallest spot was a few feet in the opposite direction. I imagined a smug smile on his face as he turned and walked toward the high point fetching a cell phone, tethered to his harness, from his pocket.

At the high point of that spire, he turned and lifted the phone for a selfie.

That was when I saw my shadow, or the shadow of the person I was in the dream, fall across the held-out cell phone and Martin Teufel's face.

I watched Martin take a step back in fear. But there was nowhere on that mountain to step back to. Martin stepped off into space.

The me in this dream counted. I counted for longer than Martin screamed or longer than I could hear him scream. After Mississippi eleven, I saw him bounce off an outcrop of rock and fall for another three or four seconds before landing in a canyon so far below I did not see the body land.

I woke to the mists on the mountain of my painting, stirring as if a storm was pushing them. When the mists stilled, the painting was the same as it had been when I first uncovered it.

I had the feeling that it was going to remain that way.

o

°

Patty Ann Calloway answered her door by calling out, "Come in. Did you dream about Martin falling too?"

I nodded.

"Let me go first," she said. Patty's dream was almost exactly the same as mine.

"Do you think he's really dead?" I asked.

"How are we going to find out?" She asked.

I called Detective John Robertson and told him that I had learned that Martin Teufel had gone to Mexico, presumably to climb. Neither Patty nor I could figure out what the mountain was that he had climbed.

Robertson said he already knew that Martin had left the country and that he was probably in Mexico. He said he would keep us informed if he learned anything.

EPILOGUE

°

Patty Ann Calloway and I got to know each other over the weeks that followed. We talked each morning on the phone to see if the other had had any dreams about Tif or Martin. Neither of us had.

We checked the news together. Patty subscribed to El Universal and other Mexican papers, and I got in the habit of stopping by her house after we both got off work and checking the day's news for any news of Martin.

I was beginning to wonder if Martin was really dead. And then one day after I had just gotten off work Robertson called. He told me the Mexican authorities had found a body in a canyon below what was known as Devil's Chisel. They were certain it was Martin Teufel.

"So he had ID?" I asked.

"They found a cell phone attached to what remained of the body," Robertson said. "The phone had been damaged beyond repair, but the memory card was readable. I have a copy of the last photos he took. If you want, you can come over, and I'll show them to you."

Patty and I went together. Robertson had the images on his computer. He sat us down, turned the iMac toward us, and left the room.

We saw in a slide show of photos that Martin must have set the phone up for multiple shots on the screen. In the first, he was looking at the camera with an empty sky behind him. But as the photos moved on, a look of abject horror crossed his face. And then the camera caught Martin in his fall. The shots ended before Martin landed.

We thanked John Robertson and left.

"Would you like to have dinner with me?" I asked Patty as we stepped out into the sunlight. "I'd rather not be alone right now."

"I'd like that," Patty said.

Just after the waiter took our order, Patty looked at me and put her hand on top of mine, which I was resting on the table. "Should I consider this a date?" She asked.

"Do you want it to be?" I asked. Her question lifted my heart which was feeling heavy.

"Yes," she said. "We've gotten together so often hoping to find out what happened with Martin; I'd miss you if I couldn't see you again."

"Well," I said. "I would love for this to be a date. I would miss you if I couldn't see you again." I thought for a moment, then added, a little frightened at what might be her reply. "Just in case we should get serious, I think I should be honest now. I don't ever want to climb any sort of mountain ever again. And I don't think I could be comfortable being in a serious relationship with someone who went off mountain climbing from time to time. The worry would kill me. So if you are going to climb, I'd rather be a friend than something more."

Patty smiled. "I swore off climbing after Tif died. You were lucky I had my old climbing harness in my car."

o

Patty and I are going to be married this coming May. And for the most part, that is the end of the story, but for one thing.

We learned this when a Missoula writer did a story about two local climbers. Martin Teufel and Thatcher Ian Febbron were the climbers in the article entitled, "Killed by the Mountains."

There was, of course, no mention of how Martin Teufel had murdered Tif. The article simply talked about both men, their climbing achievements, and their families. Tif's brother said that his brother will live on in his paintings. In it, he stood beside a painting Tif had done of Denali.

But the thing that threw us, the thing that left a dark note, was the date that was given for Martin Teufel's fall. According to the story, Martin fell on the afternoon of the Thursday that Patty and I had each, individually, awakened from a dream in which Martin fell to his death. There was no mistaking the Devil's Chisel we had dreamt about.

The article had included photos of the Devil's Chisel, another climber had taken a year or so before Martin's fall. But there was no doubt, based on the time-stamped images on Martin's cell phone still attached to his body, that Martin had fallen to his death late in the afternoon. The thing is, in the same time zone, Patty and I had awakened from our identical dreams in the morning, hours before Martin's fall.

o

The End

AUTHOR'S NOTE

Thank you for reading this book.

If you liked this book, please leave a review.

Acknowledgments

Thanks to Kaylie Burchfield's Sunbeam Editing for our final edit and Michael Lee Moore's checking our climbing facts. Nancy W. Moors for her comments. And Lee Curran for the final cover design.

A Note about Climbing Equipment and Climbing Techniques.

It may be difficult for some readers unfamiliar with climbing and climbing equipment to get a sense of what is going on in the climbing scenes.

Therefore, I offer the following subjects that the reader may like to browse.

Rather than directly linking the image, article, and video locations that could be subject to change, I'll give a list of topics to search for. I do highly recommend YouTube, as there is no substitute for seeing the aforementioned items in action.

How to belay.

How to rappel.

Tube types of rappelling devices which can also be used for belaying.

Climbing extensions.

The Munter Hitch.

Bouldering.

Pitons.

Cams
Climbing Anchors
Climbing knots (especially the figure eight)

    o

Visit if you can:
A climbing gym in your area.

    o

Articles on the subjects below will most likely be illustrated and helpful.
Common Climbing Deaths.
Climbing accidents.

    o

And books on the subject can be great references if you need to look something up to picture it clearly.
Rock Climbing For the Absolute Beginner, A Complete Guide to Bouldering, Mountaineering, Top-Rope & Trad Climbing- Includes knot tying Tutorials by K.J. Moore
Rock Climbing Mastering Basic Skills by Topher Donahue and Craig Luebben
Climbing Self-Rescue Improvising Solutions for Serious Situations Andy Tyson and Molly Loomis

If you own a Kindle or device that can access Kindle books, samples of climbing books often have a wealth of material in their sample pages, so it is not always necessary to buy the books.
Various climbing equipment can be viewed on sites such as Amazon.com.
Daisy chain extenders.
Climbing ropes— both static and dynamic
Climbing harnesses
Pitons, Cams, and other anchor devices.

Climbing shoes.

And if you get the chance, watch the 2019 Oscar winner for the best documentary movie: Free Solo. (If you are afraid of heights, have someone watch it with you that you can hold on to.)

Photo Acknowledgments

Cover Design by Lee Curran.

The ghost on the cover is by Lorado licensed from istock.com.

The mountain on the cover photo is actually one of the author's photos of Nez Perce Spire--Blodget Canyon in Montana.

At the beginning of the book, the image of the climber was made from a freeimages.com photo by 'misbass.'

The painted-over frame is by the author.

The campfire is a photo by Brian Yeager from FreeImages.com

Wedding Silhouette is a photo by Benjamin Earwicker from FreeImages.com

The figure 8 knot with a backup is an author photo.

The man climbing through a chute is an Adobestock image.

The outdoor climbing tower is an Adobestock image.

The 'pitons and carabiners' is an author photo.

The Irish pub is a combination of photos by Till Dettmering from FreeImages and Richard Simpson from FreeImages.

The image of Patty's House is a photo by Chris Lienert from FreeImages.com

The second campfire is a photo by Klaus Bernpaintner from FreeImages.com

The restaurant image is a photo by Holly McClellan from FreeImages.com

Engagement ring with moon image is a photo by Kia Abell from FreeImages.com and a photo by Otávio Brito from FreeImages.com

The photo in the climbing store is an AdobeStock image.

The photo of the cam selection is an Abobestock image.

The photo of the cam being set into a crack is an Adobestock image.

The photo of the rope being set in the quickdraw is an Adobestock image.

The wall climbing image in the climbing gym is an Adobestock image.

The Land Rover Defender image was made from a photo by Lacombe Olivier from FreeImages.com and from a photo by Paige Foster from FreeImages.com

The photo of the slanted climbing wall is an Adobestock image.

The figure 8 knot attached to the harness is a Patricia A. Curran image.

The Funeral home image is from Adobestock.

The rescue 8 device with rope and carabiner is an author image.

The graveyard image is a photo by doenoe from FreeImages.com

The cam image is a photo by the author with an Adobestock photo added.

The rope tied into an extender with carabiners is an author image.

The belay/rappel device by itself is an author image.

The belay/rappel device set up for rappelling is a Patrica A. Curran image.

The figure rappelling in the gym is from two Adobestock images.

The figure rappelling off the cliff is an Adobestock image.

The three-bolt anchor is adapted from Adobestock.

The daisy chain extender with carabiners is an author photo.

The climber is an Adobestock image.

Devils chisel is a combination of photos by Adobestock and a photo by lily rosen from Freeimages.com

The Broken cell is an image created with images by Bob Smith, and Robert Radermacher, and Armend (AD) from Freeimages.com.

www.ingramcontent.com/pod-product-compliance
Lightning Source LLC
Chambersburg PA
CBHW061248170626
46809CB00007B/2899